Heaven's Missing Wing

Nell
Weaver
Lyford

Humbly I adore thee, Verity unseen,
Who thy glory hiddest, 'neath these shadows mean;
Lo, to thee surrendered, my whole heart is bowed,
Tranced as it beholds thee, shrined within the cloud.
—St. Thomas Aquinas

Michael, row the boat ashore, Halleluiah!
Michael, row the boat ashore, Halleluiah!
—African-American Spiritual

Dedication

To Hannah Sue and George, who are there

PROLOGUE

In the first part of your life, you worry about fractions, whether or not to pop zits, what boys mean when they say something to you at the water fountain, and why you don't look as cute as the new girl in her pink and white shirtwaist.

Then comes music – for me, the Beatles, Dylan, then the Stones. Life is different, all aglow and lighter than before. People your own age speak to your inner longings, and none of your parents' sentences are intelligible. After a few more life segments, you're moderately concerned that your graduate school grades are not good enough. So you dig a little deeper into Joyce, which gives you little discernable results.

You fiddle around with a few career starts and stops. The last start clicks and you go with it. You're a real pro. Later comes parenthood, a combination of being awash in love and terrified about having enough money left over with each paycheck to put a little away for the college fund, and having to field questions like whether or not life exists on other planets. Also, what boys mean when they say something to you at the water fountain is still a distraction, although not a priority.

Soon each child must go to a top-rated college or nothing in your life that came before has ever mattered. This is the defining theme of middle age. You can play it for all it's worth if each one gets the golden acceptance letter at a college you can afford. Put the school's logo on your car. You're cool and nobody has to know you buy all your clothes at consignment stores and Goodwill. Even your underwear.

In the last bits, your mother dies a haunting death wrapped in dementia, your children become old and obsessed with paychecks and gardeners – which seems sillier than it did when you did it – and you do something called downsizing, which means nobody wants any of your stuff.

Toward the end, you marvel at how many hours a day your dog sleeps and how little you know about your husband. You drink Savignon Blanc, go to church and pray, really pray. If you're an Episcopalian, you consider confession. You decide you have too smooth of a relationship with the priest to mess it up. You write down all of your passwords and then forget where you wrote them.

You wonder about near-death experiences and talk about them over glasses of wine to your three close friends. They wonder too.

Just before it's all over, you consider who the two people are who visit you each morning. Or perhaps it's evening. Yes, open the curtains. Yes, close them. Maybe it's not every day. Is there a thing called a day? You don't know. You don't care. They seem nice.

Then you die. You don't worry any more.

This is what happened next, jumping forward in time a few years. Easy enough to do when you're dead. And yes, I can confirm there are other glorious, far-out life forms on many planets. But this isn't about that. There are also answers to what boys are saying at water fountains, but you won't find that here, either.

Everybody's story is different, so don't get all excited. And after you die, don't go looking for me to complain if things aren't like this for you. Like I said, this is what happened to me.

CHAPTER ONE

"Pardon me, Madam," said a quiet, calm male voice with a proper upper-class British accent. "You have an incoming call."

I jerked myself awake and sat up. "Hello."

"Claire, it's Helen. From school."

I swung my legs and touched the floor with my toes, flexing my heels up and down, trying to pull out of a delicious lying-in. "Helen, is something wrong? Is it Hannah?"

"No, no, sorry if this is too early. It's just that—"

"—What? Oh, Helen, if Hannah's having problems. Perhaps we shouldn't have agreed to the accelerated schedule."

"The schedule? No, it's nothing like that. Richard asked me to call you in for a little talk."

"A talk?"

There was a pause.

Hannah had never been in trouble. This was new. My wide brow attempted a frown.

"I mean, of course, when?"

"Now would be good."

"Now? Can he give me about 30 minutes?"

"Yes. I'll put you down for 9:30, shall I?"

"Sure, see you then, good-bye."

I sighed. The wide-open window by my bed glowed with a pink and golden sky, as ordered. Two peacocks were meandering around, their feathers lightly sweeping the misty ground. They cooed at each other. Funny, they never squawked.

A pink day! What a wonderful day to sit outside and sip medium-roasted coffee lattes with Laurence. Oh well. Wait, Laurence – should I tell him? No, no need. The tedium of school life bored him for the most part.

Hannah told us last night that today was an early day and she had basketball practice later this morning. Probably she lingered too long and was late for American History and Culture. Yes, that must be it. A student in an accelerated schedule must never be late: instruction moves too quickly to miss even a second.

I pulled on my favorite day gown of soft cashmere and satin. Deciding against the bronze halo with the blue, I pressed the silver one on top of my long, platinum hair. My fingers tapped the air in front of me and a tall mirror appeared. I touched the top to stretch the mirror up so that I could see all of my 5' 8" frame. Turning back and forth, I decided my angular body looked good in the pastel blue. I lifted the halo and tucked in some wayward wisps of bangs.

Entering the hall, I walked quietly and opened Laurence's door. It was dark and cool in the bedroom. His soft caramel face looked at peace as he breathed deeply in and out. No need to disturb him.

Back in the kitchen, I lifted my palm and pressed it down from the wrist, quickly grabbing the foaming mocha coffee that appeared. I sipped the sweet, slightly sticky drink.

"Comet Coffee times ten. Thank you, Cloud, this is heavenly."

"Quite literally," he said.

I opened the door, saw a taxi and hailed it to stop. As I jumped on board, I saw that the sky was now aglow with luminous cumulonimbus clouds of salmon, tangerine and azure. The taxi was a jitney, with room for several to stand. I recognized the driver from my orientation classes.

"Where to, Claire?" Johnson said.

"The school, Johnson, please."

"And what are we missing this morning, Miss Claire?"

I blushed and tapped my heart. Silver wings glided out from my shoulder blades. The others on the taxi laughed.

"What's got you so bothered, girl?" Marie, the petite black woman who lived at the cloud next door motioned for me to turn my back to her. "Let's see. Order these again, your left one is not fully spread."

I tapped a bit harder on my heart and felt both wings stretch upward and then settle into place.

I could see the school just behind a cirrus cloud. As we got closer, the Heavenly Host's ethereal music reached the cab's windows. We automatically dropped the windows to listen better.

I sighed. "Wish I could sing like that."

"Don't we all? Makes you wish you'd majored in music in college."

"College? That seems like a lifetime ago."

We both looked at each other for a moment and then laughed. Marie gave me a fist bump.

"How's Hannah?" she said.

"Fine. I think. Can't imagine why Richard wants to see me."

"He has his ways. Used to visit with him all the time when I had Tony, you remember."

"Where is Tony now?"

"Too busy to see me, sometimes he calls. I think he's still learning his job. He's working the border".

"Oh, Marie, of course. How exciting for him."

The taxi stopped quietly and hovered by the school path.

"Bye, come over some time soon."

"I will, tell Laurence hi, and that I'm happy about his sabbatical."

"Yes, bye."

CHAPTER TWO

The golden cab whisked away. I looked up at the path of gleaming stones leading to the massive ruby door, then moved to open the door as quickly as I could.

Helen stood in front of me, with large green eyes slowly blinking, her golden folds of silk falling gently to the floor. She took my hands in her own.

"Please don't worry over this, Claire. Richard always has the cherub's best interests in his heart."

"Yes, Helen, I know."

"He's waiting; let's run."

We rose a few inches up, clicked our heels and little wings pushed out of our outer ankles.

Our feet carried us quickly past classrooms and dining halls. We stopped in front of Richard's door of crystals and pearls. The gold letters on it said: *Principal, Primary School for Cherubs.* It flew open and disappeared before I could smooth out my gown. I looked up at a round face haloed in gold. Like some angels, he wasn't wearing his wings indoors, but I noted his feet wings were on. Probably to better catch a misbehaving student.

"Claire, Claire, how long has it been?"

"I'm not sure, maybe during my last guardianship?"

Richard laughed. "Surely not that long, why Hannah's been here a full year."

"Is she okay?"

Richard pulled his green and pink robe closer, and looked at his secretary. "Thanks, Helen." Helen turned and quickly disappeared, and he led me in. "Please, sit, be comfortable."

"Thank you."

I sat on a purple cushion suspended in front of Richard's desk. Another lime green cushion hovered beside it, presumably for students. And I had never noticed before, but behind Richard was a brilliantly lit shelf. Inset spotlights highlighted three golden trophies that were about four feet tall.

"Coffee?" He asked as he poured himself a cup.

"No thanks, had some earlier. But, wow, Richard. Those trophies!"

He spun around in his chair, clapped his hands and the shelf vanished.

"Oh, that, that's . . . just a little reminder of past glories."

There was a silence. Then a burst of excited children's voices.

"Class break," he said. "It won't last long. There's a contest on this week to see who can get to class first. Good prizes, candies and such. Fits in nicely with our Beginning Wings class."

I heard cherubs flitting by outside, along with a lot of tumbles, cheers, and good-natured ribbing. "Yes, I can see that."

"You never were a cherub, Claire?"

"No, I went through the Awakening at 62."

"Of course, it's in Hannah's records."

Much as I was enjoying the small talk, the deep anxiety never went away. "Why am I here, Richard?"

The slightly plump archangel took a sip of his cappuccino, then set it down. His emerald and ruby rings glittered under the crystal candelabra hanging over his desk.

Richard shrugged and opened his hands, palms up. "There's been a small . . . incident. It's puzzling and we hoped you could help."

"You mean an accident? Is Hannah hurt?"

"No, of course not, no cherub is ever hurt here, you know that."

"But what, then?"

Richard took another sip of coffee. "Sure you don't want a coffee? Oh, and there are creamy donuts somewhere. Helen baked them fresh this morning."

While Richard rummaged through stacks of paper and books, I laughed. "You mean she wished for them this morning."

Richard stopped searching and stared at me. "Of course! I know she didn't actually bake them –"

"Richard."

"–although I'm sure she could have."

"Tell me about Hannah. Please."

He closed his eyes a moment. "There was a basketball game this morning. Hannah took a tumble, lots of students on top of her. Just a general mess, I suppose."

"And. . .?"

"Hannah got up, brushed herself off and walked to the bench. That's when Coach Sally noticed."

I was breathing more quickly. "Noticed?"

"Hannah's right wing was missing."

"Missing? How can that be? Perhaps it retracted during the pileup."

"That's what Coach thought at first. But Hannah tapped many times and…nothing. It's gone."

"Did you look for it?"

"Of course, I asked Sally and Stiles – you remember Stiles, he's renowned for his vision. He happened to be refereeing and on the court."

"Yes, and–"

"No trace of the wing. It's as if it vanished."

"But . . . they don't just fly away on their own!"

Richard rested his hands on his desk and interlocked his fingers so his rings shone in my eyes. "It appears this one has. No cherub in the history of the Kingdom has ever lost a wing. I'm afraid I need for

Hannah to go home for a few days. Let me consult someone higher up the metaphysical chain. Stiles has already made a report to Corporate."

"Corporate! Oh, Richard, this is dreadful."

"I agree completely. Hannah is waiting outside the entrance door for you now. A taxi is waiting for you, too."

He rose and helped me up. I felt shaky. This wasn't happening. Hannah was such an . . . innocent. She'd made the transition when she was only three years old and life in Heaven was the only life she had ever known. One of the things I loved most about Hannah – about all cherubs – was the way they were untainted by the cynicism and selfishness those of us who had grown up on Earth had seen. And done. And now this?

"We will resolve this, Claire," Richard said. "For now, Hannah needs you."

CHAPTER THREE

A tiny form was huddled against the silver taxi – Hannah, with her hoodie up and a book clutched to her chest.

My feet flew to her and I wrapped my arms around the eleven-year-old. Hannah was one of the smallest cupids in her class and now she looked even smaller.

"Hannah, I'm so sorry this happened. We'll work it out."

The little round face was smeared with tears. I lightly pressed my fingers against them. The tears vanished at my touch, but the tight, quivering lips remained. Her strawberry-blonde hair hung loosely around her wet eyes.

"Claire, I don't know what happened. I'm so scared, let's go before class changes."

Richard had ordered us a shiny silver and white taxi. The driver took a quick look at us when we climbed in – a hooded cherub and her distressed angel – and pressed his palm against the console. A glass wall with sparkling curtains instantly shot up to divide him from his fare. He pressed his right palm forward again and a bar of lemonade and sugar cookies popped up by me.

"Thanks!" I said although I knew we were in a sound barrier.

Hannah didn't seem to notice anything. She leaned into me and the little shoulders hunched forward. I decided not to remind her that cherubs always have an open chest, shoulders back and down. Posture was not a concern now.

I gently placed my hand on the little tip of Hannah's left wing. It popped back down and out of sight. Might as well have her balanced.

Now what? Corporate? Surely not!

The taxi stopped slowly in front of our cloud. The door opened and soon Laurence was pulling both of us to him.

"What's this I hear about a lost wing?"

Hannah looked down. I motioned to Laurence to go gently.

"How did you find out?"

"How do we learn anything? Marie's cloud told our cloud that something was up with Hannah at school. So our cloud asked a cirrus cloud, since they always know everything, and it all got back to me."

"Oh, yes, I saw Marie on the taxi. Laurence, let's sit down and work this out."

"I feel like going to my room, Claire. Okay?"

"Yes, yes, I'm forgetting you must be tired. Laurence and I can sort through this. Get some rest, sweetie."

I walked with her to her bedroom. She pulled her hoodie tighter around her, even indoors. Once in her lilac and yellow bedroom, she put the book down, fell on her bed and pulled bits of the cloud covers around her. She sighed. The cloud would get warmer as she burrowed down in it.

I stood outside Hannah's room for a few minutes. I didn't think the little cherub would cry again, because sad crying in the Kingdom was unnatural. But then, everything this morning had been unnatural.

Chimes pealed as I stepped back into the living room. Laurence held up his palm to answer, waving the other at me so I'd know he had it.

"Yes, of course, Richard," Laurence said. "I'm putting you on speaker."

"Is Hannah in the room with you?"

"No, she's in bed, but I'll put up an extra layer for good measure. Cloud, we need a sound shield."

"Certainly, sir."

The room jiggled a little as the extra cloud wall rolled in.

"O.k., Richard, we're safe."

"Gabriel has all our information now."

I pushed with both hands to enter the shield.

"We understand, Richard." Laurence shook his head like he did when he didn't want me to complain.

"He says he would like to meet with Claire, and then with Hannah."

"Richard, have you ever known Gabriel to deal with the cherub school?"

"No, but this is not an ordinary event. Stiles was right; he had to be told."

"Certainly, Richard." Laurence said.

"One of his scheduling angels will contact you."

After we hung up and removed the sound wall, I took a long, deep breath. "And I thought this was going to be a real pink day."

The call came quickly. I was to report to Gabriel's office the next morning. The Great Gabriel! And me? And all because someone wanted Hannah's wing. But why? I hoped the mighty archangel would have answers.

CHAPTER FOUR

"Marie and Tony are approaching, Madam."

"Thanks." I pulled my shawl around me and brushed my fingers through my hair. "Isn't it about two, Cloud?"

"Yes. Master Laurence went for a walk. He should be home soon. He said Richard called and advised Hannah to stay home a few more days. She's watching her favorite movie."

"Thanks."

"Very good."

I dissolved the door before Marie could knock.

"Hope you aren't busy," she said.

"No, don't be silly, you're always welcome. Look, here's Laurence right behind you."

Laurence waved at Marie and Tony as he entered our front path.

When we were all settled with lemonade and coffee, Laurence began.

"We're happy you've visited us. Is this your day, off, Tony?"

"Just a later shift, start at three today."

"How's it going?"

"Yeah, I'd like to talk to you about that, Laurence."

Marie took a breath and began. "I'm the one who suggested he talk to you. I mean, you did work the border for a long time."

"And it was a long time ago." Laurence said with a chuckle.

"I'm sure much has changed – but, of course, Tony, what seems to be the problem?"

"That's it, I can't really work it out."

"Then just start from the beginning, that's what I always tell Hannah. A very good place to start!"

They laughed.

"You love musicals, don't you Laurence?"

"I love just about anything having to do with music, even the rap and hip-hop that the cherubs brought. But this isn't about me, son."

They sipped their drinks in silence for a moment.

"Here's the problem . . ." Tony said.

"Shoot."

"It's been a different few days. Hard." He placed his mug on the coffee table. "Don't get me wrong . . . I like it, it's really fun! I mean, I always wanted to speak lots of languages and now I can!"

"Hindi or Bantuu or something you never knew existed, yes I know."

"Mandarin's my favorite. Anyway, I don't know how busy it was when you were there, but lately we've had a continuous stream of angels wanting to come into the American sector. Mainly we just help with directions. Sometimes we look up where a relative or friend is, but mostly it's just should they take the blue line or the purple, stuff like that."

"Sounds about right," Laurence said.

"Guess you see so many different kinds of angels," Marie said.

"Ah."

"So," Lawrence said, "the problem is?"

There were a few seconds of silence.

"I had a strange one yesterday."

Laurence leaned in. "Strange as in–"

"Weird."

"Okay, you need to help me here, male, female?"

"Definitely male, and seemed to be dressed in a nineteenth century suit with spats. I definitely noticed the spats."

"One would. European?"

"Yes, we were conversing in what felt like . . . maybe Czech? I never really know; my brain and tongue just dive right in."

"So far you've told me nothing to merit strange. He was dressed in Earth clothes, but perhaps he's a guardian, for some reason wanted to appear to humans and just got back with no time to change."

"Except that he was more shifty than any guardian I've ever met. He avoided eye contact and at first, I couldn't understand what he needed. But he just wanted a locker, said he had to leave his suitcases at the border and that he would pick them up when he left the American sector."

"Okay. A little odd, but —"

"But don't you see, Laurence? He was traveling into the Kingdom's stateside community and yet he didn't want his luggage. I think that's a bit weird."

"Perhaps they were keepsakes he wanted to preserve but didn't need at the moment? Perhaps he decided to shorten his journey and just didn't want to be bothered?"

"Maybe."

"You don't sound convinced."

"No, I'm sure you're right, you have more experience than I do with the border."

"But . . . It is a little unusual. Maybe you could just chat him up when he picks up the bags. You could alert your peers that you want to talk to him more – they'll let you know when he comes through."

"I know. I thought of that, there's just one problem."

"What?"

"He already passed through last night when I was off. He stayed here for less than eight hours."

"What about his luggage?"

"He passed through with a new bag."

"Um . . . gifts for his family?"

"Possibly. But when a border helper saw that he had checked two bags in a locker area fairly far from the exit gate he was using, she said she'd go get them."

"And?"

"When she came back, he was gone."

"Oh."

"The locker had been empty."

Laurence shook his head. "All right, something . . . underhanded is going on. Which means dark forces at work. Which means this is something to bounce up to the archangels at the border."

I pressed my lips together. I thought I would say something and then all of a sudden, felt a bit queasy.

Tony seemed calmer after Laurence had spoken. "Yes, my partner, Francesca, and I have an appointment tomorrow."

"Good, don't worry about this, Tony. It's a little disturbing, but, I'm sure there's nothing here that can't be handled. This is Heaven, after all."

Tony finished his coffee. "Yeah, you're probably right. Sorry to bother you with this."

"The pleasure is all ours, right, Claire? Claire? You're a hundred miles away." My heart was beating fast, my stomach, jumpy. I blew out a quick breath. "–What? Oh, of course! Let me go get Hannah and we'll walk you home, Marie."

When we got back, Laurence had "The Sound of Music" cued up and pizza ready for lunch. I was still uneasy but decided to wait and talk to Gabriel. We watched "West Side Story" before dinner and later a documentary about Ginger and Fred that had been produced a few years back by Celestial Productions.

"So much to watch, and so much time." Laurence said as he shepherded us off to bed.

CHAPTER FIVE

I heard a voice softly calling me, slowly penetrating my dreams.

"Time to wake up, Madam."

I opened my eyes. My day to see Gabriel, how could I oversleep? I pulled on my robe and headed to the kitchen.

"Cloud, I need a double-shot latte." I grabbed the foaming drink.

"Thanks, is there anything I should see in today's *News of the Kingdom*?"

"I am reliably informed that God is love."

"Yes, thank you, I believe I knew that." I loved Cloud's personality, but I knew a lot of people would say 'tude. Wasn't that what my Earth ward said about such people?

"Shall I make breakfast?"

"Oh, yes, thank you."

I sat down at the smooth glass table and a mushroom omelet arrived in front of me. Toast and butter followed.

"Thanks, looks yummy. If I could just have—"

"—orange juice? Coming up."

A heavy Waterford goblet appeared and quickly filled with juice.

A centerpiece of yellow and red roses plopped down in front of me.

"Cloud, nice."

"I endeavor to give satisfaction."

Laurence came in, his red satin robe was tied with a black sash. "Breakfast, Cloud, if you please."

Hash browns, scrambled eggs, toast and jelly appeared across from me.

"Thanks, Cloud."

"Your needs are uppermost in my mind."

Laurence and I looked at each other and laughed.

"He's read way too much Wodehouse." Laurence said.

He began to spread jelly on his toast. "So, you've never met Gabriel?"

"I've seen him at Heavenly Host concerts, of course. And after my Awakening, when Jesus greeted me, I think Gabriel and Michael were somewhere near the front of the archangels present, but I can't be sure. Well, of course Michael was there...I'll never forget him!"

"No one can. But Gabriel is more . . . accessible. I've met him several times, and it's nothing to be afraid of."

"Why would I be fearful? We've done nothing."

"I meant he's not going to try to overpower you, although he could. He keeps his power more restrained than Michael. It's there, but it's less evident. Besides, it's only natural to wonder about him....what meeting someone like him, the angel who has always been seated in the highest of the high, helping God, Jesus and the Holy Spirit....would be like. Plus, he wears gold boots."

"I'm looking forward to it, actually."

We ate the rest of our breakfast in silence. When I got up to get dressed, I said, "Maybe you should call Richard and see if he wants Hannah to come in today."

"Called last night. No, he's still waiting to hear back from Corporate."

I sighed. "She'll be at sixes and sevens then."

"No worries. I have lots more Earth movies in our queue, not to mention Earth books. I still haven't introduced her to Danny Kaye."

"I know, we're all so young, Claire! I look at myself and remember when I was a young woman. Isn't it miraculous?"

"It's fun to be the same age as my parents and grand-parents. It's easier to be close with them."

"Even your ancestors from hundreds of years ago, we're all young in His service. But we must not keep Gabriel waiting."

She led down a huge hall with angels and archangels zipping all around us. I saw my guardian mentor flit by, but he was gone before I could call out his name.

"Here we are," Teresa said and waved a door away. It closed quietly behind us. The room was familiar. Then I realized, it looked like Dad's old insurance agency with wooden desks, dark green metal wastepaper baskets, a coat tree and chattering electric typewriters.

A small door opened and a tall young man with brown eyes, a strong chin and a silver ponytail entered. His dark brown suit matched his eyes. His pointy, high-heeled cowboy boots were gold leather embedded with red stones. He was reading a paper from a manila-colored file but he quickly put this down when he saw us.

"Good morning, Claire. I'm Gabriel."

"I'm pleased to meet you, sir."

"Oh, no, just Gabriel, no sirs allowed." He waved for me to sit down. "Teresa, will you join us?"

"I should like to, but I feel I must prepare for a Crossing. A daughter of an old friend is coming through."

"Yes, of course, thank you, Teresa." He watched her scurry away. "We're lucky to have her on loan from the South Asian sector. A large number of American Hindus were lost in a disaster. I knew she could help."

"It was an honor to meet her."

There was a pause as we looked at each other. I thought Gabriel's brow was exceedingly large. On Earth we would have said he looked very intelligent. I realized he was waiting for me to speak first.

"Are . . . all the Corporate offices like this?"

"No. I realized you were a little nervous and thought a familiar setting might make you more comfortable. Tea or coffee?"

"Tea, please."

Gabriel reached out his hand and pulled a teacart and service from the air and placed it between us. "Shall I play mother?" he said with a small smile.

"If you like, of course."

"Claire, I've called you here because I wanted you to be reassured our Lord is concerned about Hannah's wing." He passed me a cup of sweet-smelling tea.

"Richard told us he contacted headquarters."

"And Corporate passed it on to me."

"Is this sort of thing common?"

"Oh, no, not at all. That's why I'm involved. It's cause for concern."

"Concern?"

"She didn't just lose the wing, it was taken. We're sure of that."

"By whom? Surely not someone at the school."

"There are undercurrents at work in the Kingdom. Unhealthy angels who are confused. Dealing with them requires finesse."

"I didn't know that. But yesterday, some friends visited—"

He waved his half-eaten cookie. "—Go on, who visited?"

"Our neighbor Marie and her former cherub, Tony. They—"

"—Don't be overly concerned about this."

"But, Tony said—"

"Yes, we know what he said. And what he saw. This is all part of the disease that's working in the Kingdom."

"Surely, not Tony!"

"No, no. But his encounter. It's all related. Listen, there's no reason why you should have known about any of this. But now you've been drawn into it. One thing I should ask, have you or Laurence ever taken Hannah near the South West Gate?"

I recoiled. That place led to darkness, evil and extreme cold. It was the antithesis of all we held to be good and holy. Technically it was forbidden to cherubs, but realistically, its reputation assured that there was no reason it had to be. "Oh, no, we never go near it."

"I thought so, but I just wanted to make sure. For now, our Lord has asked the Holy Spirit to help, to stay with Hannah and help her find her wing."

"What can I do?"

"Hannah's almost twelve. We believe that's old enough to search for something so precious to her very being. But when the forces of darkness are involved, no cupid is strong enough. That's where you come in."

"How can I help?"

"Hannah must search for her wing with someone who loves her. You've been chosen."

"Of course, where do we start?"

"I have your instructions in this envelope. But please be patient with her. Give her time to rest during this journey. We have to remember she is both very young and yet almost twelve."

"I know cupids begin changing greatly when they reach the age of twelve. Laurence and I have talked about it."

"Their powers accumulate exponentially, and they begin to understand their world in a deeper way."

"Don't many cupids go on a Twelfth Year Mission?"

"Yes, this journey will replace that. Believe me, Hannah's challenge will be like few others undertaken by a cupid."

"I feel a bit wobbly."

"Nonsense, you'll be fine. Teresa has called a taxi for you, no need to fly all the way back."

I held out my hand. "Thank you, Gabriel."

He took both my hands in his. "Thank you, Claire. You are a good guardian and a good cherub parent. No need to interview Hannah. It'll only frighten her. Who knows, perhaps we'll meet again."

"I'd like that."

"Let it be a golden and peaceful day." He said as he opened the door and handed me the small white envelope.

When I came to the end of the main hall, Teresa waved for me to follow her. A small taxi hovered in the portico.

"Good-bye, Claire."

"Good-bye and thanks, Teresa."

The taxi was an extra speedy one, for I was home in less than five minutes. I decided to spend some time in solitude and prayer and slipped into our meditation room.

Plenty of time to start our search tomorrow.

CHAPTER SEVEN

"Hannah and I are going to take a little . . . outing today."

Hannah and Laurence looked up at me. Hannah seemed a bit tense, using both hands to grip her cranberry juice. She put the glass down and smoothed out the pleats in her plaid skirt.

"Where to, Claire?" she said.

"Yes, what plans have you and Gabriel hatched?" Laurence said.

I took a sip of coffee. This needed to be handled carefully. "Gabriel believes Hannah's the most likely soul to be able to find her wing. It's hers, after all."

"Where will she look?" Laurence said.

"It's not she, it's we. I'm to come along."

Hannah clapped her hands. "Laurence, too?"

I stole a quick look at Laurence, who quickly shook his head.

"This seems to be a two-female job."

"Oh, okay, if you say so."

I grabbed her hand. "Look, sweetie, this is going to be fine. The Holy Spirit will be with us. And Gabriel said we're to take this in stages and rest in between. So I imagine we'll see Laurence quite a bit."

Hannah's face brightened. "Okay, where do we go first?"

I reached into my pocket. "Here, Gabriel gave me this."

The envelope had "Hannah" in an elaborate pink cursive script. She pulled the envelope open and began to read.

"The journey is yours plus one to take.

In truth it's not a long one.

Your angel-parent must accompany you

To the center of all our songs."

"Hummmmmm. Interesting," Laurence said.

"Yours plus one?" said Hannah. "That's you and me, Claire? Going together?"

"Yep."

"Yes, that's clear, but where?" Laurence said. "The center of all our songs?"

We sat for a few minutes.

"Not a long one," said Hannah. "If I'm to come back here and rest between stages."

"The center—Corporate?" Laurence said.

"Maybe," I said.

"The center of songs," Hannah said.

"All our songs," said Laurence.

We looked at each other in realization and said the answer together.

"The Heavenly Host!"

"Of course, their cloud," said Laurence.

"Gee, sit in the audience?" I said.

"You could listen to them and perhaps one of their songs will have a clue?" Laurence said.

"They mostly sing the boring Gloria,'" said Hannah.

"Hannah! That's not all they sing," I said.

"But Hannah's right, we can ask Cloud to get a list of their program for today and see if any of their songs seem to fit in with finding a wing."

I shook my head. "No, I think we should go visit the Host. This doesn't seem like a research-from-home sort of project."

"Good luck with that."

"Why, Laurence?" Hannah said.

"Because they're always floating around on their cloud, singing."

"No, you're wrong. My mentor has a friend there. They meet for lunch sometimes."

"Really? Well, perhaps you can catch them during a meal break. I've never known any of them."

"Hannah, it'll take me about ten minutes to get ready, what about you?"

"Eight. But Claire, how can we go? I can't fly."

"We'll catch a ride. Don't worry."

She was already halfway into the hall. "I'm not worrying. I'm happy to do something."

Laurence looked to make sure she was gone, then looked at me. "What else did Gabriel tell you?"

I had intended to tell him anyway - we don't keep secrets. But I was impressed that he could see it in my face. "It seems forces of darkness were involved. But he also said that Hannah could find the wing with my help because the Holy Spirit will be with us. And that we should rest along the way. Oh, and that you were right about Tony's stranger. All part of what Gabriel called a 'disease' affecting us."

"Interesting. Hope it's not infecting us! By all means report back to me after you visit the Host. I'll be waiting."

"Pray for us."

"I already have."

Hannah ran back into the room. She had on a red hoodie to match her red and navy plaid skirt. She leaned over to adjust her ankle wings.

"Just in case we do any fast walking," she said with a smile.

I hugged her. "Let's go grab a taxi."

CHAPTER EIGHT

I asked the driver to drop us off at the back of the Host's cloud.

"Want the stage door?" she said.

"What—uh, yes, that sounds right." Actually, it sounded like a sign, and I wasn't about to ignore one of those.

We stopped abruptly at a door with Stage Door, No Admittance written across it. We got out and stood there for a few seconds.

"Hannah, buzzer."

"Right. Okay."

She pressed it, and within thirty seconds, the door opened slightly.

"Who are you and what do you want?" the Host's cloud said. For attending some of the most glorious voices in existence, she sounded like she needed to clear her throat.

"I'm Hannah the Cupid and this is my cupid-mother, Claire. We've been sent by Gabriel on a mission."

"I've received no such information. Sorry, no admittance."

The door shut.

Hannah stared at it for a moment. "I'm guessing that persistence is one of the things I have to learn?"

"Or we haven't picked the right door – Wait, I've just remembered the name of one of the Host. My mentor's friend. Let me try."

I rang the buzzer. Again the door opened a few inches. "Yes?"

"We're friends of Melinda." Actually, we hoped to be friends within a few minutes. "Here to see her."

"Ah, certainly."

The door swung open and we hurried in.

"Melinda is in the Green Room now, two doors down and to your right."

"Thanks."

Hannah opened the bright emerald green door. Small groups of angels and archangels were sitting in low lounge chairs and plump sofas, some holding sheet music and singing softly to themselves, some having tea or coffee, others reading. I asked for Melinda and was directed to an angel sitting by herself, sipping a cup of tea.

She was slightly round, short, and dressed in a yellow chenille bathrobe and matching slippers. We sat on either side of her and at first, she didn't seem to notice.

"Melinda?" I said.

She put her tea cup down and turned to me.

"Oh, sorry, hon, am I on? I thought I had at least another hour. Oh dear, I'm afraid I'm not dressed."

She rose to leave. I put my hand on her arm to keep her with us. "No, Melinda. I'm Claire, a friend of Jerry's."

She stared at me as if to get me in focus. "Jerry! I haven't seen him in donkey's ears!"

Hannah giggled.

Melinda turned to her. "A cupid! How exciting! We rarely see cupids. How are you, dear?"

"Very well, thank you," Hannah said.

"Melinda, I came to you because we need your help."

"But of course, of course. Let me guess. Do you want a special song sung?"

"No. I mean, that sounds nice, but no."

"Would you like to reserve our floating balcony? It's so marvelous, it follows us as we float and—

"Me-*lin*-da!" A large archangel rushed toward us and whipped off her gold robe and halo, throwing them on an empty chair. "Whew, I'm beat! Threading your way through a seven-voice fugue is too much for a morning."

The tall, muscular angel lifted her toes, stretching her heel wings toward the floor and her hands to the ceiling. Then she inhaled and, as she exhaled, bent from her hips, letting her hands drop between her feet. Craning her neck to look at us, she said, "Who are you?"

"Why, Victoria, these are—"

"I'm talking to them, Melinda."

I leaned over a bit to get nearer to her face.

"I'm Claire, and this is the Cupid Hannah."

Victoria inhaled up and sank into the opposite chair. "We never have cupids here."

"So Melinda was saying."

"I mean, they aren't supposed to be here. Innocence, and so many questions, and . . . they're distractions. Nothing personal, kid."

Hannah looked at me and bit her lip.

"But she's been sent here," I said. "Please tell her, Hannah."

Our corner of the room became quiet.

"Yes, dear, please do tell us." said Melinda.

"Well, you see, I lost, I lost my, my—er, my wing."

"Your wing!" Victoria said with a roar.

"Are you sure?" said Melinda.

"Hannah," I said gently, "you didn't lose it."

"No, no, I didn't. It was . . . stolen."

"Stolen!" both said at the same time.

"Yes, and she's on a journey, all sanctioned by Corporate, to find it. That's why we're here. She was told to come here."

"Wait, Headquarters? I have two letters from them." Victoria began to rummage around in her robe. "They came by morning messenger." She pulled out two card-sized, creamy envelopes. "Yes, here they are. One is addressed to me and the other to you, Melinda."

"To me! But why?"

"Read it. Maybe you'll find out." Victoria opened the envelope and began to read. "Instructions for the Cupid Hannah:

You're to go as two to look for the home,

Fly slowly, seek the one in the middle.

Its gleaming, golden dome

Will hold an essential riddle."

Nobody spoke.

"I've never liked simple rhymes." Victoria handed me the letter. "Do you know what this means?"

"Not yet," I said, "We'll mull it over."

"Go ahead, Melinda, open yours." said Victoria.

Melinda's hands were slightly trembling as she struggled to pull open the envelope. Her hand went to her mouth in a gasp as she read. She gave the letter to Victoria.

The archangels looked into each other's eyes.

"You have no choice." Victoria said.

"But Vicky, the cupid, I don't know, I've never done it to a cupid."

"What is it?" I said.

"I'm to give you an earful." Melinda said with a small voice.

"What's that?" Hannah said.

Melinda grabbed her hand. "It doesn't hurt, it's just . . . powerful. Very extraordinary to give it to a cupid."

"This is not your decision." Victoria said.

"Yes," I said. "This must be necessary for our search."

"I suppose. I'm going to pour one song, 'Holy, Holy, Holy,' into your left ear. The Heber words, to the tune *Nicaea*. Ready?"

Hannah nodded silently.

Melinda stood and shuffled over to Hannah. She tightened her robe's belt and stood squarely in front of Hannah's ear. She gently tilted Hannah's head to the right, leaned over and covered the little ear with her mouth. Then for about three minutes we heard soft whispers and low tones coming from her mouth as it moved out and in, all around Hannah's ear. Then, it was over.

"How do you feel?" Melinda said.

"Funny. Kind of . . . stuffed up."

"Yes, your ears are going to feel rather full for a couple of hours. Then you get used to it and everything's rather normal. Now for the right. This is to be, 'Are You Washed?' The Hoffman. "

"My, aren't we Baptist?" Victoria said.

Melinda looked at Victoria and shrugged her shoulders. "Someone is. Just following orders."

After she finished with both ears, Melinda knelt on the floor and took both of Hannah's hands.

"As the singer of the songs that now live in your ears, I must tell you how to release them. It is my understanding that one or both will be useful to you at some point on your journey. This is your first earful, right?"

Hannah nodded.

"If you want the song to be heard, just sing it. It only takes the first few words, about a bar, and the song becomes live again. Understood?"

"Yes, thank you," said Hannah. "Now my whole head feels tired and heavy. Is that normal?"

"Yes, you'll need to rest now." Victoria said. "In theory, you could use one of the songs during the next 24 hours, but it will be much stronger, with better harmonies and fuller orchestration the longer you wait. Two to three days should be perfect. Oh, I do hope you know these songs. You'll need to memorize the words."

"Oh, okay."

I noticed her speech was slightly slurred. "Thank you once again, both of you. But I think someone needs a nap."

Hannah seemed very groggy as we bid Melinda and Victoria good-bye and climbed into a cab.

CHAPTER NINE

Hannah took a nap while I shared all with Laurence.

When I was done, he sat and pondered things a while. "It's gorgeous outside. Let's go for a walk."

"We can't leave Hannah." I said.

"No, we'll take her with us. With a sweater on, nobody will notice her back."

"Where to?" I said, although I knew the answer.

"Why, Cloud 9, of course. After what Hannah's been through, it's perfect."

I pushed open the door of Hannah's room. Hannah was curled in a little ball on her bed, a comforter of white fluffy clouds pulled all around her.

I sat on the bed and pulled back a little cloud bit that was covering her chin. I hugged her closely and shut my eyes. We stayed that way for many minutes, gently rocking each other.

"Sweetie, let's go to Cloud 9."

Hannah opened her eyes. "Cloud 9? Is it open during the day?"

"Cloud 9 is always open."

Maybe if we went, everything would seem like a dream. A good, happy dream. I had never had a bad dream since I moved to the Kingdom. But, seeing Gabriel! As my mother used to say, Saints Preserve Us, Happy Lands!

We caught the first taxi.

"Where to?" the driver said.

"Cloud 9," Laurence said.

"Front Entrance?"

"What do you think, Claire? Do we want to stay together?"

I looked down at Hannah. She looked miserable, like a confused pre-teen on Earth.

I squeezed her hand. "Yes, we want to be together. The group entrance."

We were there in under a minute.

"Man, these taxis can move." Laurence said as he jumped out.

"Have a great time!" the driver called out as he zoomed away to catch another fare.

"What's your favorite memory, Laurence? Or maybe you'd like to show us the place you loved the most on Earth?"

Three archangels swooped by and dropped down behind us in line. Their solid platinum, diamond, and pearl halos designated their status.

"Wings in," said their leader. After quick taps to their hearts, their wings snapped into place on their backs. One of them, a short black angel, noticed us.

"Hey, Laurence! I didn't see you at first. What's up, old man?"

Laurence high-fived the archangel. "We're just like you, taking a break. This is Claire, who works as a guardian angel, and this is our cherub, Hannah."

"Claire?" said the only female of the trio. "We were in angel school together." Her curly bangs and shining dark brown locks encircled her face like a frame. "I was taking a refresher course."

"Oh, Loretta, of course. Great to see you." I gave her a quick hug.

"You can always change your mind about going for the diamonds if you get tired of guarding." Loretta said.

"I can't imagine tiring of it. I learn so much every visit. And now, Laurence and I are having fun parenting, so I'm super busy. But thanks, I'll call you if I ever reconsider."

"Claire, Laurence, this is Richard."

The dark eyes of the third archangel turned to me. I let out a little gasp. "Mr. President, so sorry I didn't recognize you."

"Yes, my apologies, too, sir," Laurence said.

Richard laughed. "I'm always not recognizing faces, even those of past presidents! All has changed – I feel so fortunate to be here in the Kingdom, with Pat, with our parents."

"I visited the Gideon Quakers several times a few years ago." I said. "My guardianship involved a man whose wife had already passed. She was raised a Friend. I thought the meeting house was quite lovely."

"Yes, it's much like what I knew as a boy."

Then the archangels nodded to Laurence and me, and we nodded back. The three encircled Hannah. They held hands and knelt down.

"Greetings, Hannah the cherub," they said in unison. "Let it be a golden and peaceful day." They quickly got up and each hugged Hannah. Then they fixed their eyes on her. The little girl stared at them.

"What do you say, Hannah?" I said.

"Thank you, thank you all." She gave each one a brief curtsey.

The group tilted their heads in the direction of the walk. With Laurence on one side and me on the other, we stepped on the walkway that was moving toward the right. The archangels each stepped on a separate sidewalk.

"I wanted to go to a Cardinal game and they have other plans," the black archangel said. "See you when you come back, Laurence."

We could only wave, for we were already in Cloud 9.

CHAPTER TEN

"Where are we going, Laurence?" I said.

"To a place I'll never forget – my first home as a free man."

I couldn't remember if we'd ever introduced Hannah to the concept of slavery. I squatted down in front of her. "Hannah, you remember that Laurence was born just before the American Civil War? To slaves on a Georgia plantation? Do you know what that means?"

"It means that people owned his parents and made them work for them. And got to hurt them if they wouldn't. Right?"

Well, she had the facts down, though I wasn't sure how much that actually meant to her.

"That's right, sweetie," Lawrence said. "But one night, my mother woke me up, told me to dress quickly and come with her. I was just five, so I didn't understand anything that happened after that, only that my father was not coming with us.

"After three days of traveling at night and hiding during the day, we met Mrs. Harriet Tubman, who counted our heads when she picked us up in Philadelphia."

We saw a 19th century street of pavement and gaslights, and then we were inside the darkened house.

"Here we are!" Laurence said. "Wilmington, Delaware. Summer, 1859. The Garretts' place."

A Victorian dining room, with dark, heavy furniture, red-flocked wallpaper, large potted palms and an enormous dining table, came into view. Mrs. Garrett and Harriett Tubman came out of the kitchen with a platter of roast chicken and two side bowls of potatoes and green beans.

"Can they see us, Laurence?" Hannah said in a low whisper.

"They can if we speak to them, but they won't remember it when we leave. It's my memory and my choice whether or not to interact with it."

Mr. Garrett picked up the serving pieces for the chicken. "Now, who's hungry?"

Laurence's mother held her five-year-old boy close to her and shrank back into the chair. I realized then that probably neither of them had ever eaten with a white person.

The archangel Laurence encouraged her. "Go ahead, Mama, you and the boy need to eat."

Everyone in the scene seemed to notice the visitors at the same time.

"Oh, Laurence, is that you?" Mr. Garrett said. "You're all grown up! And your friends, please, sit."

Laurence sat directly opposite the young boy. "You need to eat now, son, God has many plans for you." His mother smiled. Then she drew in a quick breath and covered her mouth with her hand.

"Mama, what's the matter?" the young boy asked.

"I'm just happy that's all. Happy and missing your father at the same time."

"Portia, please don't worry about him now." Harriett said. "You know we'll bring him through the railroad as soon as possible. A friend of a friend will send him."

"Your father didn't come with you?" Hannah asked.

Laurence put his arms around our shoulders. He looked first at Hannah, then at me. "Father stayed behind to protect us. He told the master we were sick the first day we didn't show up in the fields. On the second day, the secret came out and the master beat my father. But he wouldn't tell him anything."

I checked on Hannah to see how she was handling this hard truth. She seemed more confused than upset. "Didn't he know what would happen?"

Lawrence placed a hand on Hannah's head. "He did, my dear. But he was willing to face up to it because he loved us."

"Oh." She smiled. "So when did he join you?"

"He didn't, honey. He was beaten regularly after that. He died during the war, when it was almost impossible to slip through the states to freedom."

Portia sighed and encouraged the young Laurence to eat. She held out a plate for Hannah, then a larger one for Laurence and me to share. The chicken was saltier than I was used to, as were the potatoes. The green beans had a slight taste of the lard they were cooked in.

"So this is both a happy and sad memory for me." Laurence said. "But I wanted both of you to experience it. A friend of a friend sent me. That's what we said when we passed through the railway."

"I know about trains and railroads! We've studied them in 19th Century America."

Laurence's face looked tired. "Yes, of course you do. It wasn't that type of train. But it was every bit as important as the great railroads."

We finished our meal, got up, and waved goodbye as the dining scene slowly disappeared.

As we headed back to a blue exit sign, Laurence laughed out loud. We stopped walking at his abrupt change of mood.

"You know, Harriet sat by me once at a Heavenly Host Christmas concert. After that, she looked me up. She's a good friend, and of course I can see Mama and Daddy any time I like. But the most wonderful, marvelous thing, is that the past on Earth doesn't matter anymore. All that pain . . . it just didn't win in the end."

"Go Kingdom!" I pumped my fist. Hannah giggled.

"Do you feel better, Hannah?"

"Oh, yes, thanks. But I still want my wing back."

"We do, too."

Laurence and I looked at each other. I had eaten too many pota-toes. All I wanted to do was to head to Hannah's nearby bedroom and unroll her cloud comforter.

"Sleep with me, Claire?"

"You're reading my thoughts. Sure."

CHAPTER ELEVEN

"The Cherub Tiffany approaches." Cloud said.

"Yeay!" Hannah burst through the front door.

I smiled. Tiffany, with her blunt-cut coal dark hair and almond-shaped eyes, was Hannah's best cherub friend. Like Hannah, Tiffany had died as a toddler and was being brought to maturity here in Heaven. They were at about the same level of development, just gaining that awareness of suffering you needed to form compassion.

Seconds later, Hannah led Tiffany inside. "Can we do smores, Claire?"

"Smores?" Tiffany said. "What's that? Is that something to play with?"

Hannah laughed and covered her mouth. "Smores are to eat, silly."

"Okay, okay, I'll bet my angel-parents do things yours don't do."

"Yeah, like what?"

Tiffany sat cross-legged on our couch and paused for a moment.

"Well, I know how to call hogs."

Oh, no! I had forgotten Jeff, Tiffany's cherub daddy, went to the University of Arkansas in the 1950s and was an absolute sports fanatic. When we first met, he learned I had lived in Little Rock, so the Arkansas Razorbacks' football and basketball teams were all he could talk about. He recently arranged to be a guardian for an assistant football coach so he could go down to Earth for any game.

"What are you talking about? Who wants to call pigs? Like on a phone or something?"

"Watch!" Tiffany sprang up and jumped to the side, her front knee bent, the other leg draped behind her. She leaned over her knee and then raised her arms above her head, back arching dramatically, hands shaking wildly toward her back foot. "Wooooooooooooooooooooo, Pigs, Sooie!"

More hand-shaking. Same crazy moves and yell. Now her hands shook up and down her body for the third call. "Wooooooooo, Pigs, Sooie!" She jumped up and shouted. "Razorbacks!" To cap it all off, she bounced up into a big split jump. No varsity cheerleader on Earth could have done better.

Hannah was stunned. "What was that?"

Laurence ran into the room. "What in tarnation?"

Tiffany proudly crossed her arms over her chest. "That was calling the hogs. Jeff taught me."

"Very good, but I suggest you take any yell leading outside. We don't want to upset Cloud."

"Noted and appreciated, sir," Cloud said.

With this, Laurence left the room.

"That was really good, Tiffany. Maybe you could teach Hannah. And Laurence has a friend who was a cheerleader at Dartmouth in the 1920s. They were yell leaders then."

"Yell leaders?" Both girls laughed. Hannah did a little jump. "I want to learn!"

"Let's go to your back yard. There's more room and we can jump better. You have to really bounce up and not use your ankle wings."

"Okay. Smores later."

The door slammed shut. Laurence joined me on the couch and we both started laughing.

"I used to make a lot more noise than that," he said. "Now I know why my mother sometimes just threw up her hands and asked for God's guidance."

"But they're having so much fun, Laurence."

"I know. I remember."

We read for about thirty minutes while the girls yelled and jumped up and down outside.

"Madam?"

"Yes, Cloud?"

"The girls seem to be tiring. Would you like the fire lit?"

"Excellent idea."

"And I've located four long pronged sticks that appear to be suitable for roasting."

"Super. Thanks, Cloud."

Soon we were poking our sticks of marshmallows and chocolates over the fire.

"Claire? Hannah said her Earth-dad was a senator."

"Yes, he had just been elected to the state senate when he had the accident."

"My Earth-dad was an insurance agent. Who's more important?"

"Well, I'd say your dad was more important if you needed insurance, and Hannah's was more important if you needed laws. Why?"

"Just wondering." Tiffany looked at Hannah and then into the fire.

"We're just . . . trying to work things out." Hannah's voice was quiet and far-away.

CHAPTER TWELVE

The morning sun was at the midway point across the eastern sky. I was enjoying my late breakfast and coffee.

Cloud cleared his throat.

"What's that, Cloud, do you need something?"

"Oh, no, Madam, just wanted you to know a security van is humming its way to our door."

"Security? Who is it?"

"The great Michael."

"Michael! I'm not dressed."

"If you take the opportunity now to get presentable, I'll open the door and serve refreshments."

"No, that . . . shouldn't . . . I'll hurry."

I dashed to my bedroom and pulled on a pale pink silk as I heard Cloud announce Michael.

"Coming!"

I slowed to a fast walk. "Michael, so marvelous to see you."

"Claire, it's always pleasant to see you and Laurence. Is he here?"

I indicated for the archangel to sit on one of our most comfortable chairs. "No, but he should be back soon, just out for a morning fly-around."

"I may have to miss him, then. I'm afraid my time is limited. You can share my news."

"Of course. Coffee, Michael?"

"No, thank you."

This was the closest view I had ever had of Michael. He was almost as tall as Gabriel and, like him, Michael presented as strong and muscular. I quickly took in his white suit, white shoes and silver socks. The last time I had seen him was at an Easter sunrise service. Then he was dressed in traditional archangel garb with one smart addition—a gold breastplate.

"We have a Crossing scheduled for tomorrow."

"Who?"

"Joe."

Joe. When I had died, my husband was still in fairly robust health. Now it seemed it was his turn. I took a deep breath and then let it out. "Will he be alone?"

"Yes. His body is eroding. That's why we know 24 hours or less."

"I've never managed a Crossing before, but I know Joe will be expecting me."

"He will. But don't forget, you'll have his mother and father and anyone else you feel should be there. Some of them should have experience."

"I'll have to think, of course, his older sister is here."

"Regina, yes."

"Are you involved with the family before every Crossing?"

"Yes and no. Peter and my office work together as the awakened one travels to us. I make the transfer to loved ones once family members are in the river. You remember."

"So, you took the time to tell me personally. That's kind of you, Michael, you have many duties."

"Well, I felt the need to talk to you. We're putting extra security on this, during his passage and once he enters the river we'll—"

"—On Joe? Why, what's he done?"

"Joe, nothing, he's just a sick person who needs to come home."

"Then what are you afraid of?"

Michael stood up. "I, personally, am not afraid of any man, woman, angel or archangel. Our Lord keeps all who believe and trust in him safe. However, chaotic and highly unusual things are afoot. Hannah's stolen wing is an example of that."

"Hannah and I visited the Heavenly Host."

"Yes, I heard. The earful. It's powerful protection."

"I know we have to continue this search, but Hannah is so vulnerable. She isn't even twelve."

"I hope my visit hasn't alarmed you."

"Confused may be a better word."

"When chaos and evil are about, confusion . . . typical."

"Evil? Here?"

"I can say no more. We're keeping extra security on you, your cloud family and earth relatives. Vincent is in charge of earth protection. He's a highly trained warrior against Evil, and he's watching over all loved ones on Earth. As for our Kingdom, you won't know we're there. But I almost forgot, please report at noon to the Crossing's production room. You'll be able to plan a perfect welcoming experience for Joe. We have very able angels eager to help."

"Thanks so much, Michael."

"Not at all, Claire. I hope Joe's Awakening is everything you could want for him."

"I'll make sure."

Michael opened the door with a small wave of his hand. "Let it be a golden and peaceful day. Take care."

"Thanks again."

But I wasn't sure Michael heard me, for as soon as he stepped out of our cloud, he unfolded his magnificent gold wings and zoomed straight up beyond my sight.

I sank into a chair. "Well."

"Most intriguing." Cloud said.

"I hope I can remember everything – just the way he said it."

"I took the liberty of recording the scene, just in case."

"Cloud, what would I do without you?"

"Possibly a subject for later reflection. Pardon my intrusion, but will you bring Master Joe here?"

"I hadn't thought about it. Need to see what Laurence thinks."

"He's hovering outside, having a chat with the lugubrious head gardener. Expectations are that he will be at the door in less than a minute."

CHAPTER THIRTEEN

"A silver and gold coach awaits outside for you, Madam." Cloud announced a bit louder than usual.

"Wow." I adjusted my halo in the mirror.

A four-seated coach, with four white horses, a type of taxi I had never seen before, hovered outside. A driver dressed in gold robes and wearing goggles motioned for me to hop in.

"Hello, Claire. I'm Arthur, I'll be your driver all day."

"Thanks."

In what seemed like only a minute, the coach was stopping in front of a large multi-windowed building with Gothic arches. It was set in a forest landscape and reminded me of the Thorncrown Chapel in the Ozarks.

Its two massive doors opened to reveal not pews but tables and chairs. A redheaded angel, her halo tilted back to keep her curls from tumbling onto her forehead, rose to meet me.

"Claire, hi, I'm Nancy. Josh and I are producing Joe's Awakening and Crossing."

"Thanks so much, I feel a bit lost."

"Oh, no sweat. Josh and I have done hundreds of these. Michael calls us sometimes when a boomer is coming through. We had a production company on earth."

Josh — I assumed it was Josh — was in a discussion with a larger angel, but when he saw me, he crossed the room. He was shorter than Nancy, with a warm, glowing tanned face and huge brown eyes. He put his hands around mine. "Claire, nothing to be concerned about, piece of cake."

"I'm sure. But this is my first to manage."

"You leave all the logistical stuff to us, let's all sit down and talk about how you want this to look and feel for Joe."

"Forgive me, but when I came through I . . . uh, I don't remember much until my mom hugged me in the river."

Josh leaned back in his chair and tapped his fingers together. "That's fairly common. It's a big transition. . .can be overwhelming."

"Familiarity is the key," Nancy said. "So let's just take it from the top. Who should he see first?"

"At the river?"

"Yes, don't worry about earlier. The soul's passage from Earth to the Kingdom is run by Peter and Michael, according to our Lord's wishes."

"Well . . . his parents and my parents need to be invited."

"We have their names and cloud addresses, just wanted to con-firm their participation. Your parents as well?"

"Oh, yes, Joe was very close to them."

"Any siblings, children?"

"His older sister, Regina, is here. Yes, we need to invite her."

"That makes six of you. We recommend keeping the number to nine or under. And we believe Joe should see you first, then his own parents."

"We should be fine with those relatives and me."

"Great! Now let's think about music."

"Mahalia and a big choir brought me in. I had difficulty absorbing that, but Dad told me later that it really was Mahalia."

"But this is Joe's. So what does he like the way you liked old gospel?"

"Joe is a cradle Episcopalian and didn't grow up with any of that. He likes show tunes and big orchestras."

"His file has show tunes, Mormon Tabernacle Choir, The Talking Heads, Everly Brothers, Beatles, and Beach Boys as favorites," Nancy said. "Also, 'West Side Story.'"

I felt the unusual sensation of tears in my eyes. One of the angels taking notes handed me a handkerchief.

"Let's consult the availability list." Josh said and tapped on a laptop screen. "We need to stick to mid-to-late 20th century performers. Let's see…our version of the Beach Boys is on vacation. John may be available. It's possible he could get George to come. But no, I see they couldn't make our deadline."

"Phil and Ike are booked for a crossing taking place right now and then one later today," Nancy said. "They're always game, but we don't want to wear them out. How does Elvis sound to you?"

"The Elvis? That would be amazing!"

"Most things here are. He told me yesterday he's available all week. He sings with Aaron."

"His twin? I've never seen them perform. How does it work?"

"Just as well as Elvis did on Earth, only better." Nancy said. "Their voices create breath-taking harmony – if Joe likes the Everlys, they'll be perfect. If you want them, we need to schedule right now, because the river is busy at the moment. A lot of boomers are coming through."

"Yes, definitely."

"They have about 100 songs in their repertoire."

"Elvis used to sing, 'Precious Lord, Take my Hand.' I always loved that. Used to sing it around the house and Joe would comment that it was unfortunate my voice was so bad."

"Got it, what else?"

"It would be nice if Elvis did a solo, especially 'Maria.'"

"Good idea, plus I see that's your middle name. Claire Maria, very nice."

"Could we have a big orchestra sound?" I didn't want to be too demanding, but this was Joe's Homecoming. And he only got one.

Josh ran his finger down the availability list. "Lenny is free this week. We'll contact him, with your permission. They practice together every day, so he can put the orchestra together in about fifteen minutes."

"Lenny?" I felt I was losing it. Was this really happening?

"Yes, this will be perfect." Josh said. "He wrote the 'Maria' lyrics, you know. Everything will work out."

"How do you want the river to look?" said Nancy.

I took a sip of water that an angel quietly placed in front of me. "Ummmm. I know you can do lots of special lights and such, but, really, if we have Elvis and Aaron on the banks singing, and the orchestra, seems like it should look fairly natural."

"We have to have a bit more guidance." Josh said. "The River Jordan appears differently to each person. As the leader, you'll set the scene."

"Well, we took a Colorado canoe trip once, lots of whitewater, then calm pools."

Nancy was typing away at her pad. She turned it toward me. "How's this?"

The pad showed a lush, mountain valley with a clear river running through it. "Beautiful, perfect."

"Okay, team, let's go with this image. And place a willow tree near the best entry point so Claire will have a landmark to look for."

An angel sitting at the table stood up and looked at the picture. "We're on it." She left the room.

"Do you have a time for this?" I said.

"We should. Peter's staff told us anytime within the next 24 hours, and that was about 6 hours ago." Nancy said. "So we can't dawdle, but we should be good. Let's go through the plan.

"First, your relatives have been alerted and should be in the green room within an hour. We have plenty of food and drink there, lots of sleeper clouds, they'll be comfortable. We need you there as soon as we wrap up this meeting."

"Okay."

Nancy opened a folder and read from it. "Here's how this unfolds. We give you a heads up when he's one hour away from the river. This should give you plenty of time to get ready."

"Are we dressed as angels? The reason I ask that is I don't remember my mom looking different, except that she was younger."

"You'll enter the river—remember to go to the willow tree and wade in there—and by the time you reach the halfway mark, all of you will be in earth clothes he's familiar with. It will feel very natural to you. As soon as you see Joe, start calling his name and reaching out to him."

"Yes." said Josh. "This crossing is under special security alert. Peter and Michael have stressed to us how important it is for all of you to say Joe's name."

"Doesn't that happen in every Awakening?"

"You'd be surprised." said Nancy. "Some relatives just sort of freeze when they see their loved one. Anyway, you won't do that. By the time you've brought him to the home shore, Joe will have his wings."

"This is so exciting! I haven't seen Joe alive and feeling young in so long."

"That's why we enjoy our work so much." Nancy said. "We'll have you all on the screen behind you."

I turned and the wall immediately changed into a screen. A running screen saver message said, "Praise the Lord, for He is good."

"Okay, what happens then?"

"That's up to you. Where do you want to live, at least on a temporary basis?"

"I'm in Zion now, with a cherub and a friend."

"We recommend you stay with Joe in a more private setting until he gets his bearings. Also, during the first 24 hours, our Lord will visit him. God works 24/7 and besides, as Christians, Jesus will want to greet both of you."

"So," said Josh. "Pick Zion, Beulah Land, or Gilead. Nancy is partial to Beulah."

"I've visited it and it's certainly gorgeous. Cirrus homes seem larger, and there's more space between them."

"Oh, please join us as neighbors! All of my husband's family, mine, and some of Josh's family are there. Josh lives in Zion, but that's because so many musicians are there."

"Okay, you've talked me into it, but I need to tell Laurence and Hannah."

"Cloud," said Nancy.

"Yes, Ma'am, what may I do for you?" said a calm, yet upbeat female voice with a Midwestern sound.

"Tell Claire's Zion cloud that she and Joe will be living in Beulah, at least for a while. And explain the timing of this Awakening so they won't be concerned about Claire."

"Consider it done."

"Thanks, Cloud."

We heard a ringing tone that sounded like many harps strumming through a chord.

Nancy reached into the air and pulled out a phone. "Yes, here . . . Yes, of course we'll be ready . . . Thank you, Peter." The phone disappeared. "Peter says go to the green room. Joe is coming over in about two hours."

CHAPTER FOURTEEN

A big archangel who had been quiet until now slowly stood up. He had a large face and twinkling eyes. I remembered him from guardian training. "Okay, Claire, ready to make this happen?"

"We'll see, Fred."

"Come along."

The angel gently took my hand and led me to a door I hadn't noticed. I turned to wave good-bye to Nancy and Josh. I hated to leave the gorgeous place, and yet, I was so eager to see Joe.

The door opened and there were my parents and Joe's parents, George and Olivia. Then another door opened and Joe's sister, Regina, came in. Regina looked as amazing as always, dressed in a classic angel gown sprinkled with diamonds and pearls.

The four parents were dressed more simply in Earth clothes and yet with a few added touches, as if going to a party. Olivia wore her pearls. George had on a familiar blue and gold bow tie. Suddenly, everyone was standing and engaging in multiple hugs and tears.

"I'm so happy, aren't you excited, Claire?" said Regina.

"Beyond excitement." We hugged for a long time.

"Hey, let's order you a special gown."

"Okay, I didn't know things were going to move this quickly."

"Cloud, please send in some diamond, pearl and emerald gowns for Claire."

"Certainly, anything else?" said the deep bass voice of the green room's cloud.

We all looked around the room.

"There's plenty of food and wine, so I think we're okay." Olivia said with a little laugh.

"Anything I can do for you before I go back to help another family?" Fred said.

"We're fine, thanks." But I didn't feel fine. I tried to calculate what time it was in Little Rock, whether or not William and Sarah might be at Joe's bedside. Would they know it was time? That he was dying? Death was not that bad if it was happening to you. But it was so hard on the people who were left behind.

But I couldn't think straight, couldn't work out the earth time. Knew I needed to focus on the moment.

"Good luck to all of you." Fred said as he waved good-bye. "Let it be a golden and peaceful day."

I watched him leave and sighed. "I'm having a hard time processing this."

Regina frowned. "That sounds like Earth-talk."

"I know -- no whys, whats, hows, right?"

"Not even when, except . . . it does seem soon."

We hugged again. I loved her for understanding.

"Madam, the gowns are in the changing room," Cloud said.

"Thanks."

"I'll help." Mom said.

"Sure Mom, help me unzip this." We moved behind the screen.

"Goodness, these are spectacular." There were so many ornate gowns crammed on the rack, it reminded me of the bridal gown reality shows I used to watch on Earth.

"Oh, Mom, I'm so excited, I can't think!"

"It will all work out, darling. We're all here for you and Joe."

"You look good, Mom, I like your hair."

"It's funny. I used to wear it this way when your father and I first met, long before we were married." She looked in the mirror and patted her chignon roll. "And now, I love having it again."

"One and one-half hours to go." Dad called out in his booming voice.

"Mike, let Claire at least try on these dresses in peace!" Mom rolled her eyes at me in the mirror as she finished zipping me up.

"Right, folks, let's get some grub. It could be some time before we eat." Dad said.

The five of them were around the buffet when I stepped out in a long, pale blue gown. The sleeveless bodice was satin and the skirt was encrusted with diamonds and pearls. "What do you think?"

"Beautiful!" they said all together.

"Thanks, I think I'll have a small glass of wine."

Dad poured me a Sauvignon Blanc.

Soon bells pealed. One hour to go.

CHAPTER FIFTEEN

I led us out of the green room door. We immediately stepped onto the Kingdom side of the river. It was spectacular, just as Nancy had shown me. But I was trying to focus on getting everyone to the right spot.

An archangel with long blonde curls hovered beside a willow tree, her wings just brushing the branches. "Come," she said and we walked to her. "Just to review, when the clouds break and the light comes through, you immediately step into the water. Go toward the light."

I took some deep breaths. Regina reached out for my hand. We all adjusted our clothing. Mom knelt down to take off her heels.

"Don't worry about shoes, you're all going to find yourself in church clothing in the river."

Mom stood up and shrugged her shoulders. Then she gasped and pointed to the growing hole in the stratus clouds.

"Go," said the archangel.

As it turned out, in the beginning, I never heard Elvis, Aaron, or the orchestra. I was surrounded by soft, indecipherable sounds as the water rushed over my ankles, then my knees.

Two archangels zoomed toward us, zipping through and out the ever-growing tunnel. Our family was directly in front of the almost over-powering light. It temporarily blinded us so we all looked down, blinked a bit and then stared once more into the tunnel. Then I saw him—Joe!

"Joe, Joe, here, we're here!" I called out.

All of us started calling and then shouting his name. We could see him now, walking slowly toward us, looking a little stunned. He was in blue flannel pajamas, his old wool robe flapping around his legs, and a glowing light encircled his entire body.

"Joe, come to me, come to the river!" I splashed my way to grab him. He faltered, we embraced once, and I pulled back briefly so the others could see him, but he grabbed me and we held each other tight. He looked about 30, and in between hugs, I let out a little gasp when I saw him again as he once was. I had forgotten.

I gleefully led him to his mother and father, who embraced him. Then it was my parents' and Regina's time. There was a lot of shouting and cries of happiness.

"I–I can't believe this. Is this a dream?" Joe said slowly.

"Nope," I said. "This is real. Before long, what happened on Earth is going to feel like the dream."

We stood in a circle, holding hands. Except for Joe, we were all dressed for a Sunday morning on Earth. It felt very comfortable to be in this family circle. The haunting echoes of "Maria" could be heard.

Then, suddenly, Michael zoomed through the tunnel.

"Down, everyone!" He instantly spread his giant golden wings over us and was quickly joined by four other archangels who did the same.

We leaned in together, peering at each other through a dim light, since their huge wings blocked the scene's bright sun. Regina was frowning, our parents looked startled. I could tell Joe was frightened.

"What's going on?" I asked Michael, whose face sternly hovered over us.

"Yes, what in blue blazes–"

"Mike, hush–"

"Olivia, I just wanted–"

Michael drew his fingers to his mouth to silence us. There was a loud swooshing sound and the tunnel closed abruptly, causing the river water to jolt and ripple.

After what seemed like an hour – probably just a few more minutes – Michael nodded to the other angels and they released their winged roof. We slowly stood up, still holding hands. One by one, the archangels turned and flew up to the top of the willow tree.

I looked up at Michael and he spread his arm, his hand pointing toward the bank.

"What was—"

"It's okay, Joe, follow me." I led our group out of the water, and we held on to each other as we slogged our way to the shore.

"Joe, good to see you, man." Elvis nodded from his cloud stage. He and Aaron glittered in gold lame. They put their arms around each other's waist and began"Precious Lord."

"This is . . . You're sure this isn't a dream, Claire?"

I held Joe again as I felt Heaven's clothing and wings back on my shoulders. "Does your dream have wings?"

Joe laughed, "Is that what I feel on my back?"

Mom waded through the last of the water. All of the family was in angel-wear now. "You'll get used to them in about a day. Claire will show you how to deal with them."

"Where to, now?" Regina said.

"After whatever that was, I'm for a meal," Dad said. "I just barely touched the green room's fare."

Olivia pulled down her gown that was slightly bunched around her ankles. "Joe needs to go home with Claire. He won't be hungry for the first day or so. He'll have a special visitor soon."

Joe stared at them. He squinted, then blinked several times and reached for his mother's hand. "Mom?"

"Yeah, we're all young again." Dad said. "So how about the rest of you? I hear the new Gilead Diner has great food. Our Lady gave them some of her favorite recipes."

"Lead the way, pal." George said. "We're going to see much more of you, son, but your mom is right, now is the time for rest."

"Let me hug my little boy once more before he goes." Olivia held Joe close and kissed his cheek before joining the others.

The five of them rose slightly, wings beating slowly, then one by one they went higher, forming a line of angels headed to a safer flying height. Their good-byes filled the sky. Joe stared after them and actually giggled a little.

After we couldn't see them any more, Joe said, "How did they do that – I mean, I can't believe . . . Claire, I just saw my parents fly away!"

"Don't worry, we have a taxi waiting for us." I looked around and decided the nearest cloud was the stage manager. "Cloud, we're ready for our coach."

"Certainly, it's approaching."

The gold and silver coach zipped up on the shore and made an abrupt stop in front of us.

"Welcome, Joe." Arthur adjusted his goggles as we stepped in. "Where to?"

"Our new home in Beulah." I said. "Nancy made all the arrangements."

"Right-o," Arthur said. "Hold on because I sense someone needs a lie-down. Heard you had a rough landing back there. Maybe a good stiff drink, privacy, whatever fills the bill."

"I . . . do feel dizzy, is this normal?"

"Regina told me she passed out on the shore. Your mom and dad had to help her into a taxi. And yes, Arthur, privacy would be great. But no drink yet."

"This is a taxi?" Joe said when we were underway. "We're flying! And angels—all sorts of different colors and wings! And I see more angels flying down there with children. Wait, the kids have wings! And that amazing sound, what is it? Where is this?"

"It's the Heavenly Host singing, darling. Welcome to Heaven."

CHAPTER SIXTEEN

The coach sped through the air. Joe put his head on my shoulder, and I put my arm around him. I hugged him, then took a deep breath. Joe did the same. "I'm keeping my eyes closed on purpose."

"Good idea. But you'll get used to it, faster than you'd imagine. You're finally home."

We felt the coach slowing down. I looked out at our new cloud. Our home was in the middle of a cul-de-sac, with other edgy, cirrus-styled cloud homes on either side. The homes were glowing softly in shades of pale blue, orange, pink, and violet.

Like most of the Beulah clouds, ours was long, wispy and slightly flat. Its many rolling indentations caught the afternoon light and reflected back gentle rainbow hues.

"This is it, folks." Arthur jumped out and opened the door. "Need any help?"

Joe slowly opened his eyes. He blinked and looked at Arthur, then at me. "I don't know, do we need help?"

"We're fine, sweetie. Just slide across the seat and step down carefully. There, I've got you."

I held Joe's hand as he stepped on a patch of grass suspended in the air.

"Whoa! How do we walk?"

"Just walk, the air will support you." I dropped his hand and walked around to show him.

"Amazing."

"Well, if you two are fine, I'll say good-bye."

"Thank you, Arthur."

The driver waved as he pulled the horses around to head back toward Zion.

Shooing away the two peacocks that were standing in the stone path, I slowly led Joe inside. Helping him sit on a sofa, I propped his feet up on an ottoman.

"The inside of this house seems fluffy, soft."

"It's a cloud. Everyone lives in one."

"Oh, I see. Of course. No, not of course. Why?"

I sat down across from him. "I don't really know. Tradition, I suppose. Would you like to lie down?"

"Boy, feeling a tad wobbly."

"I'll crawl into bed with you, I'm feeling a bit weak myself."

We made our way to the first bedroom where an enormous bed awaited. "Um, cloud covers. You're going to love these."

"Wow, fantastic!" Joe kicked off his sandals and lay down.

Soon I could hear his rhythmic breathing and knew he was asleep. I turned toward him and watched him.

"Madam," said our new cloud in a low whisper. We had a female cloud with a soft, yet authoritative voice. That could be fun. I had never lived with a feminine cloud sporting a proper BBC accent.

"Yes?"

"John the Baptist and Mary Magdalene are approaching."

I got up quickly and pulled on my slippers. "Thanks, Cloud."

I opened the front door just as the two visitors arrived. I waved them inside with a small bow.

"John and Mary, this is an honor."

John waved it away. "How is Joe? Heard there was a bit of trouble at the river."

"He's resting, thanks."

"Does he seem feverish?" Mary said.

"No-o. I don't think so, but I hadn't thought of that."

"It doesn't matter. We're here to prepare the way for our Savior."

"I was told to expect Him."

"He visits all Christians who have crossed over. We came to your parents' house and saw you."

"I remember, thanks."

A thin, round beam of white light shot through the open door. It slowly grew larger and larger. We knelt.

I stayed on my knees as the light moved into the bedroom where Joe lay. I was vaguely aware of John and Mary getting up and following.

It seemed like just a few minutes had passed when Mary Magdalene was gently shaking my shoulder.

"Claire, Claire, Joe needs you now. He will want to tell you about Jesus."

"Has He gone? How long was He here?"

"About an hour. They talked of many things. Our Lord placed oil on Joe's face, head, and heart to renew him after his passage. He will be much better now."

Mary helped me up. "I'll ask your cloud to make tea. And John left *The Guide* for Joe."

I hugged Mary. "Thank you so much, for everything."

"All in our Lord's service. Now go."

I turned and jogged toward the bedroom. I found him sitting up in bed. He had pulled out some pillows for his back. We hugged.

"Do you want to talk?"

Joe's face was shining. His breath was slow and deep. "Not now. Will you help me think about what just happened later?"

"Of course, Sweetie! Oh, and I have a book for you. John left it. It will answer a lot of your questions."

"Claire, that was Jesus just here. Jesus!"

"I know. It kind of hit me in waves for the first few days."

"I can see that." He picked up the book. *The Guide for The Awakened Citizen, American Christian 21ˢᵗ Century Revised Edition.*

"And, here, look! John signed it."

We looked at the inscription.

"'For Joe. Love, John.' Very nice, very kind of him."

"I think I'll read a bit of this now. I'm bursting with questions."

"Cloud has tea and scones for us. Cloud, our tea, please."

A teacart appeared beside the bed. Maple, pumpkin and cranberry scones were stacked high. A silver teapot and two Blue Delft china cups and saucers were placed beside the platter.

"You remembered I like tea time! And that's the pattern Regina collected. Thanks, and if I haven't said it yet, I love you."

"Ummm. Actually Mary Magdalene ordered it. But I love you, too."

"Will I ever feel normal here?"

"Absolutely. And *The Guide* will help."

"I want to at least look at the Table of Contents now. Don't be bored, but I want to read this page and perhaps you can comment on what I should read first."

"Sure, go ahead."

"The Crossing, Your New Home, and under that is The Cloud System. Then Orientation, Visiting Earth, Advanced Flying and Overshadowing, and Your Role in the Heavenly Country. We have a role here? You mean like a job? I thought we just . . . relaxed, maybe got some fishing in . . ."

I flopped back, trusting Cloud to have a pillow waiting. She did. "I know, it surprised me at first, too. I guess that, after working for decades just to have finally saved enough to take time off, but then after you quit your job, you get sick and die, an eternity of doing nothing and having people wait on you would have seemed like heaven.

"But really, the best thing, the most joyous thing, is to share God's love. And that means doing things to help others, to make them happier, to serve them in some way. That's your role."

Joe thought about this for a moment. "Okay . . . let the greatest among you be a servant, that sort of thing?"

"Exactly. Some sing in the choir. Some, like Arthur, drive taxis. Anything that lets you use your own gifts to help others."

"So what's your role?"

"I'm a guardian to a guy on earth. Also a cherub mother." I didn't give him a chance to jump in with a question – I knew he would, he always did, it was so nice to be talking like this again. "When someone dies while they're still immature, they can't simply be transformed instantly into adults. They wouldn't be themselves. They have to grow up here. I'm taking care of a little girl, she's eleven going on serious questions."

"That sounds . . ." He gave me a huge smile. "You always were good with kids. And a guardian – like Clarence and Jimmy Stewart?"

"Something like that. But I'm thinking about handing him off to someone who really enjoys being a guardian. Being a cherub mom has been much more consuming than I thought it would be. Guess I'd forgotten about the early years!"

"So what do you think my role will be?"

"I don't know, but there's no rush. You do get to relax some." I tapped the book in his hands. "Anyway, since you probably don't remember much about your Crossing, just start in the beginning."

"Okay." He flipped the book open. "Was my time in the river normal? I mean, that circle with those big–"

"Joe, there are many things happening. I want to share them with you, but you need to rest first. And while you're reading, I want to check on my cherub. She's been having a hard time, lately."

"You won't be gone long?"

"No, I'll be back in about an hour. Oh, and an old friend wanted to say 'hi'."

"Who would–"

But before he could ask, our beloved black and tan shiba inu, Rose, ran through the bedroom door.

"Rosie! You little dickens!"

Rose spun around clockwise, woofing with excitement. Then she reversed, still barking. To conclude her arrival, she jumped on the bed and landed in Joe's arms.

"How did you find her?" he said as he alternated between hugging the little dog and scratching between her ears. Rosie quickly licked his face.

"She found me a few days after I arrived here. But Laurence doesn't like house dogs so much, so I told her to go back for a while until we could all be together again."

"Laurence?"

"A good friend. All in due time. Rose's been with her mom and dad. They were all in our old breeder's home in Zion – you remember Josephine. She passed through before me. I've visited her and we've gone on long walks with Rosie and her whole dog family."

"Of course I remember Josephine. I'm so happy to see Rose. And she's so young—just like you."

"You might want to check yourself out in a mirror. And now I'm going to leave you with your book and Rose."

He gestured toward our dog, his book and the teacart. "I definitely have enough to keep me busy!"

I grabbed a scone and took a quick sip of tea. "If you need anything, just ask Cloud."

"Uh, sure, but I'd rather you did that for now."

I laughed. "Skip ahead and read about the Cloud System. It will give you courage."

He grabbed my hand. "I have courage because you're here. But do you have to go just yet?"

I leaned over and kissed him. We held hands, sitting quietly, for several minutes. I let Rose give me a few face licks. Then I gently pulled away.

"Okay, okay, I know you need to leave. Your cherub and all. I'll be fine."

"Cloud."

"Yes, Madam?"

'Help Joe if he asks for you. In fact, help him even if he doesn't ask."

"But of course. I am here for him. Go on your way and don't fret."

CHAPTER SEVENTEEN

I caught a taxi to Zion. Within a few minutes, I was knocking on my old door.

The green door evaporated after one knock and Laurence stood in front of me. He gave me a long hug. "We've missed you, Claire."

"Things have been crazy. There was trouble at the river."

"Trouble? What happened?"

"Not sure, but Michael was there. I can just stay a few minutes. Joe is understandably weak and a bit confused. I left as he was starting to read *The Guide*."

"Oh, that'll really confuse him." Laurence laughed and indicated for me to sit.

"Good afternoon, Madam."

"Hi, Cloud, how are you?"

"Much improved with your presence. May I offer you a latte?"

"Of course, yours are the best in the Kingdom."

"Service is my pleasure, my lady."

I grabbed the coffee suspended in front of me. A table appeared, laden with coconut and chocolate chip cookies.

"Cloud, you remembered how much I love these Brown Sugar cookies."

"How could one forget? The little bakery truck near your old Earth residence concocts some of the most divine cookies on that planet. And

I don't mean to be presumptuous, but when should I prepare for you to come home, Madam?"

"Oh, Cloud, not anytime soon, but thanks for missing me." I turned to Laurence. "I think Joe and I need to be alone for a while, but I wanted to make sure you were okay with this. I can take Hannah if you want, but I don't think it's good—"

"Don't worry about it. I love Hannah! I'm happy to be her angel support for now. She's such a sweet little cupid, why would I want her to leave?"

"Thanks."

"And how are you? Maybe a little confused yourself since you learned Joe was coming?"

". . .And yet it all feels right. John, Mary Magdalene, and our Lord visited us."

"I'll bet that helped Joe."

"And overwhelmed him a bit. But he slept after that, and I think he's already much calmer."

"You've said so much about him. I'd like to meet him."

"I know, but first I need to tell him about you."

Laurence tilted his head, held it in his right hand, and looked at me. "And what will you tell him?"

I sighed. "I'm open to suggestions."

"Try to explain how love is different here."

I grabbed Laurence's hand. "I know, I want to do that. Pray that he'll understand."

"He will, then we can all be together. It'll work out."

I reached into my pocket and took out the note Melinda had given Hannah. "First, I could use your brains on this one."

"Another instruction?"

"From our Heavenly Host visit. Listen to this:

You're to go as two to look for the largest home,

Fly slowly and seek the one in the middle.

Its gleaming, golden dome

Will hold an essential riddle."

Laurence took the note and studied it. "The largest home, that could be anywhere. Heaven doesn't build small."

"It's discouraging."

"A golden dome, though. Couldn't be many of those around."

"No, I've been trying to remember where I've seen one."

"Some churches? The Greek and Russian Orthodox go for onion domes."

"Yes, but this says home."

"Yes, home…"

We didn't talk for a few moments.

Then he rapped the note with his knuckles. "The Castles!"

"Of course, that must be it."

"There's a new structure, right in the middle of the complex. Remember where there was a large courtyard?"

"Vaguely, I only visit Jamie, and he lives on a corner."

"Yes. Well, this is a new domed structure, I've seen it on a fly-about. It's a gleaming, golden one. Must be it."

"I think we should go tomorrow."

"Yes, I'll have her ready. What time?"

"I'll pick her up about nine."

"By the way, the latest report came in, and her grades are really good. She got an A in four-wing flying and a B+ in hovering—the teacher considered how well she was doing before she lost the wing. The other grades come out in a few days."

"Wonderful! Hovering is tedious, I'm proud of her."

"It's an exercise in patience. Of course, we had a celebratory chocolate shake with those marks."

"Let me go leave her a congratulatory note as a surprise."

"Oh, I almost forgot, Marie stopped by."

"Really? She's kind, probably thought you'd be lonely. Did you tell her Gabriel knew all about Tony's border experience?"

"I told her to tell him not to worry about it any more, that Corporate had it all under control."

"Ummmm, maybe…"

"She was more concerned about Hannah, spent an hour or so talking with her and letting Hannah show her all her school books. That reminds me, the science fair is in two months."

"And I thought that was over when you left Earth."

"Apparently not for cupids. And learning to see theoretical structure and elegance behind everyday life is one way to grow."

"Did you just say something about theoretical structure?"

"Why?"

"Have you ever gone through this ordeal with a student?"

"No, but I thought the elegance–"

"Stop right there. This is a grind from start to finish, okay? On Earth it seemed to last for four years. Just tell me what her topic is."

"Something involving wing speed. Not really sure….vague at this point."

"Yep, and it will be until we get involved. Oh well, let me go check out her room."

When I opened Hannah's room, a strange smell hit me. "Ugh, what's up with this?"

Fanning my nose, I wrote a short note and then pulled the door shut. I found Laurence flipping through some history books.

"Laurence, perhaps you'd like to go to some presidential seminars with Joe and me."

"Maybe. Who's speaking?"

"George, Thomas, John, Teddy and Franklin. I saw it in the paper. I know Joe will want to go. Meeting historic figures will help him get used to being here."

"The Roosevelts, definitely. I've heard they do a really good job. I'm kind of burned out on our American forefathers. I know Thomas and George have acknowledged their great mistake, but . . ."

"Understand. By the way, what is that awful odor in Hannah's room?"

"I know, it's tough isn't it? Marie brought Hannah this disgusting . . . perfume? But Hannah likes it, thinks it's cool and very big girl, so Cloud and I are practicing our tolerance."

"It's awful. Tell her I said I'd bring her a nice scent when we get together."

"I'll tell her, but I'm not sure you'll talk her out of this one. It's like the more she puts on, the more she thinks she needs to put on. Honestly, cupids!"

"Remind me to tell you about Axe body spray some day. You said you were okay with taking care of her. This seems like a lot. Are you sure?"

"Sorry, I was just indulging myself in a generational outburst."

I gave him a hug. He smiled and waved me away. "Go, I've kept you too long. Let it be a golden and peaceful day."

I nodded.

"Farewell, Madam. Don't be a stranger!" said the melodious tenor voice.

"I could never be, Cloud."

I reached out and we hugged once more.

"Claire, Claire, I do miss you, but I know now your place is with Joe."

I stepped back. "Yes, for now, certainly. It's confusing. I love Joe, of course, but we—"

"We were very happy together here with Hannah. But things change here, just as on Earth. You must give this time."

I stepped outside the door. He followed me and took a deep breath.

"A little breezy, but all in all a great day for flying. See you tomorrow, I'll have her ready!"

I rose, circled and waved to my dear friend.

CHAPTER EIGHTEEN

I had just taken off my lace poncho when Joe called out, "Claire, is that you?"

"Yes, coming."

I lay beside him on the bed. He reached for me and I snuggled down on his chest. Rose jumped up with us.

"How's the *Citizen's Guide* going?"

"I decided to just ask you questions. When I read, I feel like this is all a strange dream. I mean, basic how-to flying and how to treat your cloud – unreal."

I kissed his cheek. "Shall I pinch you?"

"No, but give me a big kiss, that should do it."

We kissed, hugged, and kissed again.

"Okay, feels like your old kisses. Not like dream kisses."

I laughed.

"Have you had anything to eat besides that scone?"

"No, and I'm ravenous. What do we have?"

I shrugged. "Anything you want. Cloud will prepare it."

"Good grief – then yes, Cloud, I would like an omelet and a side of bacon."

"What kind of omelet, Master Joe?" Cloud said.

Joe hesitated – it was hard to get used to having a servant if you'd done for yourself all your life. I nodded encouragement.

"Uh, cheese and onion, please."

"Coming your way."

A tray table settled in on Joe's lap. A large omelet and a thick slab of maple-smoked bacon joined a small pink rose in a crystal bud vase.

"This smells delicious, thank you, Cloud."

"Anything to drink, sir?"

Joe turned and whispered to me. "Do they have mimosas here?"

He was so serious, I tried not to laugh. "Yes, very good ones."

"A mimosa, please."

"Two, Cloud."

Two tall flutes appeared on the tray. Joe took a sip. "Delicious!"

"Thank you. Will there be anything else?"

"No, Cloud, we're fine for now," I said.

"I can't get over this cloud system."

"Did you read about it?"

"A little. Is it a computer?"

"Not computers the way we knew the concept on Earth. All the clouds in Heaven are networked together to meet angels' needs. It's a bit like a butler, cook, personal assistant, concierge, tour guide—you name it. You'll get more comfortable with it as the days pass. They are amazing and very helpful."

"So, no cooking in Heaven? You must love that."

"I do, but it doesn't have to be that way. Regina cooks most of the time. Her cloud gathers recipes and ingredients for her some of the time, sometimes she shops."

Joe took a bite of bacon. "Yes, I can see that, she always loved to cook."

"She'll have us over soon. I'm in the habit of going there at least once a month."

"Time . . . works the same here?"

"Yes, typically we have hours and days in synch with Earth."

"Why's that?"

"Not really sure. Must just have evolved that way. I know in the beginning days, other things were organized quite differently."

"Such as—?"

"Like the neighborhoods. We live in an American community. Most of our neighbors are Jews and Christians from the 20th and 21st Centuries. But if we wanted, we could live with Japanese from the 10th Century in the Japanese community who practiced Shinto and believed in Buddha - I met him once, by the way. Think it's just worked out that people are more comfortable with some familiar references, touchstones to their former life."

"Yes, I guess I see that."

"But Laurence, my friend I've lived with for the last few years, is in this sector and he's from the 19th Century."

"American?"

"Yes, and you'll be fascinated by his Civil War stories. He was born a slave."

Joe stopped eating, put down his fork and looked at me. "What does that mean?"

"Only that –"

"Seriously Claire, you with him—living together? I know you came here first, but... I don't know, I didn't see a chapter on this. How do all the Earth marriages work up here? We're together now. Was that a decision you made?"

"So many questions! Laurence and I met, and our friendship became strong enough that we wanted to live together. Think about it this way: you could have remarried on Earth."

"But I didn't."

"Oh, I know. This is something else you're going to discover on your own, but I'm going to try to explain: love is different here."

He was already calming down enough to listen. He never could stay mad for long. "In what way?"

I took a sip of my cool drink. The champagne was still fizzy. "It's hard to describe. But you're going to find that you feel the same about everyone."

"I'm sorry?"

"I mean, that . . . no that's exactly what I mean. The longer you're here, the more you're going to feel an emotion that you can call love or friendship or whatever, for just about everyone you meet. Even when you meet someone who has a slightly difficult personality, you'll find that doesn't really matter."

"I haven't seen anything in the book about this."

"As I say, it's a little hard to explain."

"I still feel weird about this Laurence guy."

"Okay, I understand and I want you to meet. But first, I have to tell you about a mission I'm on."

"They have missionaries up here?"

I laughed. "No, not that kind of mission. Here's what's happened." I took another sip of my drink. "Right before you came, my cupid, Hannah, had her right wing stolen."

"You're kidding, right? That sounds absolutely crazy."

"No, I wish I were."

"But crime in Heaven?"

"I know, it's highly unusual. And Corporate—"

"Corporate?"

"—is involved. That's where all administrative and other major decisions are made. Gabriel works there."

"Oh, Gabriel, right, I should have known, okay, go on."

Joe rolled his eyes and I could tell he thought this was a joke. It would help if he could meet Gabriel.

"Gabriel told me that Hannah has to find the wing herself. But that evil forces were involved, and that as someone who loved her deeply, I'm supposed to go with her on her journey."

"Claire, is this some crazy test you've been asked to give me during my first 24 or so hours up here? I mean Gabriel really existing and talking to you and something evil stealing a little cupid's wing? Cupids and cherubs are the same, right? Sounds . . . unheavenly."

I nodded.

"I wish this were not real, but it is. The event at the river, right after you came through—that happened, right? That was not normal. Families don't usually cower under the wings of archangels waiting for the tunnel to close."

"I thought it was scary. But I was pretty well off balance myself at the time."

"Joe, we all thought it was scary. But this is what I'm trying to talk to you about—abnormal forces are at work. I must be with Hannah as she searches for her wing. Somehow, her wing is part of this."

Joe put down his mimosa, wiped his mouth and sat up straighter.

"All right, if you're involved in something like this, I want to go. It sounds dangerous."

I smiled. "I knew you'd say that, but you don't even know how to fly yet, and we have to press on as quickly as we can. Hannah and I have been to one of the destinations, received further instructions, and are headed to the Castles tomorrow morning. We'll be perfectly safe there, I assure you."

"The Castles? That I remember. The formerly homeless, destitute, down and out, disa . . . um . . ."

"Disabled, yes, Jamie's there. I'll see him tomorrow."

We hugged for a very long time before turning out the lights.

CHAPTER NINETEEN

Hannah was sitting outside, reading a book, when I lowered my wings and settled down beside her. She had on a heavy sweater that hid her wingless state. The faint scent of Marie's awful perfume was present. I hoped it wouldn't linger.

"Ready?" I said.

"Yes, Laurence told me where we're going."

"Can't remember. Have you been there?"

"We went to the Castles on a field trip last year. It was so beautiful!"

"Yes, it's pretty spectacular." I spotted an empty small taxi and waved it down. As we approached the shiny towers, our driver had to duck and weave the car to avoid hitting the increasingly heavy traffic. He waved his hand disparagingly at some of the stretched cars.

"These limos, honestly." he said. "All these Castle people love them."

"Guess it does make for some tricky maneuvers." I said as we swooshed around a silver Rolls.

"Aw, nothing to it, really." he said. "I flew a SPAD for the Lafayette Escadrille. This is kind of fun."

He pulled up rather abruptly by the curb in front of an enormous, glittering gold staircase. It led to gold and silver gates that stretched up about thirty feet. Two angels, dressed in luminous, flowing robes, stood on either side of the gates. One of them had a notebook.

I leaned close to Hannah. "How are your ankle wings these days?"

"Good, I can go up."

"Great, let's go."

We glided together up to the top.

The taller angel stepped forward. "I'm Robert. May we help you?"

"Yes, are you expected?" said the other, a female with a blonde-streaked ponytail pulled through her halo.

"I'm Hannah and this is Claire."

The female checked her list. "Sorry, but I don't have you down. This is the Castles, maybe you were looking for another place?"

Hannah looked at me and I motioned her on.

"Well, we do have business here. Perhaps Gabriel—"

"Gabriel!" said Robert. "He put us on this duty, just this morning. Maybe. . ."

Then I heard a familiar voice calling from behind the gates. "Oh, Robert, Robert, dear. Please do be a sweetheart and let my guests in."

A raven-haired angel appeared just behind the gate. She was dressed in a long, flowing lavender dress and wore silver and purple sandals.

"Of course, Liz. I didn't realize they were here for you." Robert pushed the gates back.

"Hey, Liz, next time, just give us a call and we'll know to expect any guests. Are they here to see Marge?"

"Well, yes, thanks, darlings." Liz said with a wave at the security angels. Then she stepped between us and put her arms through ours. "Hello, my dears. Extra security on our gates for some reason today. I'm Elizabeth. But call me Liz. You must be Hannah and Claire."

"Yes." Hannah said and peered up at her. "You look so much like the girl in 'National Velvet.'"

"Oh, that old thing," Liz said with a laugh, then leaned down and stared into Hannah's eyes.

"But I am, darling. I am that girl."

"Wow. No wonder the Castles are awesome!"

"Yes, aren't they?" I said. But I wasn't looking at Liz, I was staring at the magnificent courtyard upon courtyard, all covered in gleaming mosaics. And there was the golden dome.

"Let's have tea outside, shall we?" Liz said. "I look after Marge. She'll be coming down soon. I believe Gabriel asked her to assist you."

A few minutes later, Hannah was sipping on her chocolate malt, and I stirred sugar into my tea.

Liz leaned back into her chair. "Good to stop for a while."

"You work here?" I said.

"Sure. You know how the Castles are run."

"I don't." Hannah said.

Liz leaned over and tucked a lock of hair behind Hannah's ear.

"Well, my darling cupid, the very poor and downtrodden on Earth get to live like royalty here. It's a beautiful life for them and helps make up for the life they lived on Earth. You see, if you live your entire life with everyone treating you like you don't matter, it makes you feel yourself that you don't matter. Living like this . . . " She gestured to the breathtaking courtyard. ". . .helps heal that. And those of us who lived like kings and queens on earth help take care of them, which is also good for us."

Hannah was still looking around her. "How come?"

"Hannah came here when she was about three years old," I said quietly.

"Oh, you poor dear," Liz said. "So you don't know your parents?"

"Claire and Laurence are my angel parents."

I squeezed Hannah's small hand.

"Well, you know how your parents enjoy taking care of you? It makes us feel good to make someone else happy, someone we care about. And Marge is really remarkable. She's so kind – and so fascinating."

I glanced down at Hannah, not sure how much of this was going over her head. I was already forgetting that there was hardship in the world, and I'd only been here a few years. For someone like Hannah who grew up in Heaven, what did being poor even mean?

"Maybe you could tell us a little about her." I said.

"Well, her family was very well-to-do in the early part of the 20th Century. They had a big house with servants. Lived in New York. He was a judge. Then came the crash."

I looked at Hannah. She had the same look on her face she did when she hit a tricky homework assignment.

"The Great Depression." I said. "The stock market crash in 1929. A lot of people lost all their money."

Hannah nodded. "Right. Money. We're going to review that next month before our exams."

"Well, I've got a real live example of someone who lived through it, honey." Liz said. "Her dad left them, made her mother divorce him so he could marry some floozy with a little money and eventually drank himself to death."

"How could someone die from drinking? Do you mean he drowned? And what's a floozy?"

Liz looked up at me and smiled. Hannah had been asking more and more questions like this one lately. I'd been getting more confident at coming up with answers.

"Well, Hannah," I said slowly, "a floozy is a woman who's kind of . . . sad. And her sadness makes her . . . cling to other people and do things that . . . hurt her and everyone else. And another thing sad people do is drink alcohol."

"You mean wine and ale and stuff? I thought that made you happier."

"A little bit does, yes. But some people, when they're very sad, drink so much that it hurts their bodies."

"Oh. So there were a lot of sad people on earth."

"Oh, yes," Liz said. "Anyway, Marge and her mother struggled on. Marge worked as a clerk in a factory for a long time to support her mother – that's a really hard job. Then her mother died. Marge lost her job and soon after, dementia began setting in."

"That's a disease that makes you forget who you are." I said in an aside to Hannah. She seemed shocked but didn't say anything.

"That's when I first saw her."

"You knew her on Earth?" I said.

"Well, yes, as much as I knew any homeless person. When I stayed at the Carlyle in New York, Marge was usually stationed around the corner from the entrance. Sometimes she had a shopping cart, sometimes just a big plastic bag."

"What was in the cart?" Hannah said.

"That's the thing. Everything she owned."

"Oh, that's right." Hannah said. "They don't have clouds on Earth. At least, not like we do here."

"That's right." Liz sighed. "One Christmas, I was there visiting friends. We were all feeling particularly giddy that evening and walking arm-in-arm, probably laughing about the latest Hollywood or New York gossip. We were warm, happy and headed for a great meal. Then I spotted Marge. She was sitting in the little recessed doorway she used to get out of the cold, her newspapers pulled around her feet, and a blanket around her shoulders. She didn't say anything as we passed, just seemed to stare ahead."

"Gosh," Hannah said. "No wonder people were so sad. What did you do?"

"I'm afraid nothing at first, pretended I didn't see her. We hailed a cab. But then when we got to the restaurant, I still kept seeing her huddled against that building. So I called my assistant. Told him to take my fox coat and a hundred dollars to Marge - that was quite a bit of money then. Didn't know if she'd take it, but she did. I mean, how many dead animal coats do you need? I had several."

We both shrugged.

"From that night on, I always brought a gift of some sort to Marge when I was in the city. She wouldn't let me help her more than that. She wouldn't ever take food, but she would take cash and clothes." Liz closed her violet eyes for a few moments and then took a sip of tea. "Then I was at the Carlyle in the early nineties, and she was gone. We tried to track her down, but it was no good. I learned after coming here that she had passed through soon after that—died, as we called it on Earth. The police had found her lying in her little spot, in a coma -"

"That's so sick you stay asleep all the time." I whispered.

"Right," Liz said. "Anyway, she lived the last few days of her life in a hospital bed. At last, someone was taking care of her."

"Liz! Where are you?"

"Over in our favorite courtyard, dear, please join us."

Liz stood up and walked over to meet a short, brown-haired angel dressed in a lemon satin gown. Her bangs almost covered her eyes. Liz carefully brushed them back and tried to tuck them behind Marge's ears.

Marge batted her away. "Oh, it's no use, honey. You know I like my bangs long."

Liz pulled out a chair for Marge.

"Liz, how many times do I have to say this? I'm perfectly capable of sitting all by myself."

Liz quickly sat back down. "I know, Marge, darling, but you know I love fussing over you."

Marge looked at Liz's beaming face. "Oh, I know. And I love you for it, Liz."

"And I love you, darling. Now, this is the little cupid Gabriel was telling you about."

"Pleased to meet you. And you're Claire?"

"Yes."

"Liz fix you all up with food?"

"Oh, yes, Miss Marge." Hannah said.

Marge laughed a hearty laugh. "Miss Marge? Nobody's called me that in a long time!"

We all sat smiling at each other. I decided to break the silence.

"Marge, Liz says you have something for Hannah?"

"Right. It's here."

She pulled a small, crimson velvet sack out of her pocket and handed it to Hannah.

"Should I open it now?"

"Why, sure, hon, we're all friends." Marge said.

Hannah untied the gold sash, reached into the little pouch, and pulled out a small key. It appeared to be platinum and had diamonds inlaid all around its border.

"How beautiful." I said. "What does it open?"

Marge looked at Liz and they both looked at us.

"You tell her, Marge." Liz said.

"The great angel asked me to part with my most precious possession—that was easy. It had to be my first key to my Castle home. My first home in so long."

"You see, Hannah," I said, "on Earth, most everyone had a door with a lock and a key. It was a way to keep your possessions, the things that made your life comfortable, safe."

"So other people wouldn't . . . steal them, right?" she said. "Like my wing was stolen?"

"That's right. But Marge didn't have a key for a very long time. This is very precious. Best keep it safe in its pouch."

"Oh, almost forgot, it came with instructions." Marge handed Hannah an envelope.

Hannah opened it and read.

"This Place was made by God

And yet it's very near to Evil.

Take the key to its neighbor, but be wary.

Dress warmly, sing together and don't tarry."

Hannah looked at me as if I should interpret.

I shook my head. "Sorry, kid, maybe Liz or Marge can help."

"Not I," said Liz.

"Nope, me neither."

"We'll work it out, Hannah. Laurence always has good ideas. Now I have a favor to ask of you two."

"Shoot." said Marge.

"I'd like to visit a friend here. Could I possibly leave Hannah with you for a few minutes?"

"She can stay as long as she likes." Liz said.

"Sure, why don't we take her back to my apartment?" said Marge. "It's in the eastern part of this building. The views are terrific, and my cloud makes a mean chocolate cake."

She pointed to the middle building with its golden dome.

"I'll find you." I said. "I won't be but just a minute."

"Do you know how to find your way?" Liz said.

"What? Oh, oh, yes. See you in a bit. Thanks."

With that, I was using my ankle wings to zip down the courtyard, up the first entry hall and then the second.

Before long, I was standing in front of an elaborately carved wooden door. Feeling something I rarely felt in heaven. Fear.

CHAPTER TWENTY

I knocked. No answer. Knocked again. The door vanished and a tall, blonde-headed angel having a bad hair day stood in front of me. His eyes were sleepy, like he had just gotten up from a nap.

"Oh, hi, Miles."

"Hi, Claire."

"Is he here?"

"Yes, come in, please."

I stepped into the magnificently appointed suite. Its walls of soft caramel suede complemented the slouchy, low, navy-tufted satin sofas and matching chairs. Gigantic rock and roll posters of bands from the sixties through today were sprayed all over the walls. I was particularly taken by the day-glow colors of the Jefferson Airplane one.

"Please, sit," Miles said. "He'll be out soon."

I sank down into one of the chairs, my elbows almost in my face. I looked around. Their cloud needed to dust, but I wasn't about to suggest it.

A muscular, dark-haired thirty-something came out of a bedroom. He quickly pulled on a t-shirt, raising his left, then his right shoulder to push his wings through. His frayed jeans dragged across the floor as he moved closer.

"Hi, Claire."

"Hi, Jamie."

"Coffee?"

"No, I can't stay. Just wanted to say hi."

His brown eyes stared intently at me. "Okay . . . "

I got up. "Jamie, Joe came through."

"Yeah, I heard."

"You did? How—"

"GiGi told me."

Of course. Mom would have told him. "He'd like to see you."

"Yeah, sure. He knows where I am."

"Actually, he doesn't. I mean, he doesn't even know how to fly yet."

"Yeah, well. He's smart. He'll learn."

I didn't want to reply.

"I'm really kind of busy now." he said.

"Oh, yes, so sorry. I was near here and wanted to say hi."

He was staring out of the gigantic window wall that overlooked the courtyard. "You said that."

I walked toward the door. He didn't move.

"Well, take care of yourself," I said.

"I always do."

"Yes, well, bye for now."

He held up the peace sign.

I returned it and left through the open door. It shut quickly behind me.

I stumbled a bit turning a corner and caught a glimpse of my face in a mirror. My face was dark. I had never seen this in Heaven, and paused to take some deep breaths. After I counted three breaths, my complexion was back to normal.

I had to get back to Hannah. We had many things to share with Joe and Laurence.

CHAPTER TWENTY-ONE

Hannah was sleepy when we returned home.

"Could I take a nap, Claire? I stayed up late last night."

I nodded as she left the room.

Laurence looked a tad sheepish. "We watched six 'I Love Lucy' episodes."

"Six. That's three—"

"I know, I know. But it's a good, innocuous way to introduce her to Earth concepts. And she does enjoy them so much."

"Veeta, vita, vegamin?"

"Of course, and the candy factory with Ethel. Some when they go to California - the one with Harpo Marx. All hilarious."

I sat down on the sofa and he took a chair. "I used to watch those over and over."

"So you understand, and won't give us a hard time."

"Just don't want her to get tired. She needs all her energy for this."

Laurence nodded. "What did you learn at the Castles?"

"I'm not sure."

"Tell me."

"First, security was tight. I didn't tell Liz and Marge, but it must be about the wing."

"Who are Liz and Marg?"

"Marg spent most of her life destitute and living on the street. Liz, former glamorous actress, takes care of her."

"Have I seen this Liz in anything?"

"Have Hannah introduce you to 'National Velvet.' And we could do the 'Taming of the Shrew' sometime. You'll enjoy it. Anyway, the key's tiny, fashioned from platinum and diamonds. She has it in her pocket."

"We best find a chain for it so she can wear it around her neck. This sounds important."

"Yes, I left some necklaces here. She can choose one."

Laurence nodded.

"Mom was offered a place there, you know."

"No, you never told me."

"Thousands of former slaves live there. It was too grand and overwhelming for her."

"I can see that. And yet—"

"—Jamie's there."

" I saw him."

"A good visit?"

"No more than always."

"Oh, Claire. Want to talk about it?"

"Not now. But you can help me with the letter Hannah received." I pulled it from my pocket and handed it over.

He read it slowly and gave it back to me.

"'This place was made by God.' Hummmm, that doesn't narrow it down much. But there's something . . . 'This place was made by God.' This place was—

"This place—locus iste. Locus iste. . ."

Laurence moved quickly to a group of books in the middle of shelves behind the sofa. "Cloud, have you seen my *Heaven's Special Places for Touring, Revised Edition?*"

"It should be immediately to the right of *The Archangel's Role in the Kingdom*," Cloud said.

Laurence ran his fingers over several books' spines. "Got it, thanks."

He pulled out a large bronze leather book, then sat beside me and spread it on his lap so we could share it.

"I love all these illustrations." he said. "The Hudson River School at their best."

He scanned the index and then flipped to a page. "Here. *Locus iste a Deo factus est.* This place was made by God."

I stared at the painting of an old Celtic monastery. Two male angels in brown robes stood outside, beaming at us. *Locus Iste a Deo Factus Est* was carved in the stone archway over the door. There was a tremendous starry night surrounding them.

"I think you've got it. Where is this place?"

"It says right here." Laurence began to read. "'The mission stands in the outermost corner of Heaven. Pilgrims are welcome, yet are warned that the journey may be difficult. No public transportation is available. Therefore, any angel traveling to the mission must fly. It is recommended that no angel attempt this trip alone. The mission's diamond sky setting is unique in Heaven.'"

I broke in and continued to read. "'Care should be taken to avoid overshooting the monastery grounds, as the South West Gate lies a few miles to its west.'"

Laurence slowly closed the book. "That's what I thought."

"Near the South West Gate, scary." I leaned back into the sofa. My heart was beating a bit faster and I pressed my lips together. No, "scary" wasn't the word. I was petrified.

"You'll have to be more than careful."

"I don't see how I can do this with just Hannah—it's overwhelming to think about it."

"You won't be. I'm going with you."

"Not sure that's allowed."

"Claire, Hannah can't fly, and you can't possibly carry her that distance."

"You're right. But I don't know what to tell Joe."

"The truth is always good. But make it quick, we should leave early in the morning."

What had I gotten myself into? But Laurence was coming with us. Surely that would help.

"Guess I could be here about six, early light."

"No, we'll come to you. Joe needs to meet me and Hannah."

He was right, no more putting this off. "Okay. Tomorrow then."

"Dress warmly."

We hugged.

"Until then." I said and soon I was lifting off toward Beulah.

CHAPTER TWENTY-TWO

I flew home at a lazy pace, rehearsing how best to tell Joe all that had happened since I left him. I was even trying out different lines, looking for the one that would be most reassuring. But then it hit me–where was my faith? The same faith that I had learned to rely on during my time on Earth, why should I ignore it now? Of course, this was a journey required by God and we would be supported by Him. Faith – our belief in God's grace – would get us through. I started to feel physically better, like a giant stone had been taken off my chest.

When I could see our Beulah cottage, I settled down on a nearby cloud. I landed near a peacock that fanned its feathers back and forth and flew a few feet away.

Lying on my tummy, I picked a few mauve and lime cloud fluffs and stared at our cottage. So, how to tell Joe I was leaving on a dangerous trip without him? With Laurence? I sighed. I must encourage him to draw on his faith, too. Realizing this was the only way, I said a prayer, stood up and flew down. Soon I was walking through our front door and Joe stretched out his arms to me.

"Joe! What's up?"

"I am. Decided I'd been lazying around too much in bed. Besides, Regina called and she's coming over tomorrow for dinner. Thought I should go over some menus with Cloud. Glad you're back."

"Regina has always cooked for me, even when she's at my place, just like she did on Earth. Don't worry about it."

"Oh, okay. Does she order ingredients in advance?"

"No, if she wants to eat, at say, seven, she'll get here around six and start working with Cloud. You'll see, it all works out."

"Looking forward to it. Guess we should invite Mom and Dad. Oh, and Rose just trotted out the front door like she knew where she was going."

"Don't worry. She's just checking in with her dog family. She'll be back soon. But let's sit down. I need to talk to you."

"That sounds serious."

"I'm afraid so."

We settled on the couch. I took his hand.

"Joe, you know how happy—how joyful—I am to have you here."

"But. . ."

"We seem to have perhaps one of the last clues in the search for Hannah's wing. Maybe it is the last one. We don't know, but we're very close."

"Good news. What happens now?"

"Hannah and I need to take a journey. We'll leave early tomorrow morning and probably be returning in two to three days."

"Why so long?"

"Because we're going a fairly far distance, but the main thing is we'll need to fly part of it, so it'll go slower."

I looked at him and he pressed his lips together. "Okay, I sense there's another 'but' lingering here."

"Joe, I'm going to just tell you, but please don't be mad."

"Go. Tell me."

"I need Laurence to go with us."

Joe looked at me for a few seconds. "Why?"

"Hannah can't fly, remember?"

"But why him? And where in God's name are you going in Heaven that you can't take a taxi or bus to? That doesn't sound right."

"We're going to an old monastery. It's . . . near the South West Gate."

"What? I just read about that. You can't go there! I mean, you aren't supposed to go there."

I took in a breath and blew it out. "I know, it's a problem, but the clue leads us there. The monks who serve the mission can guide us. They'll know the best way to deal with this."

"I don't know, Claire, this sounds way out of control. Way too dangerous."

"I'm going to pray tonight. I hope you'll do the same. We need to find the wing, Joe. But we need to be prayerful about it. It's not something we can do on our own."

"I'm going to talk with Cloud." Joe said.

"Please don't bring her --"

"Cloud, have you been listening to this?"

"Only in a dispassionate way, Master Joe."

"What do you think? Should Claire do this?"

"Joe, pe—leeeeze! Cloud isn't privy to all the details."

"If I may interject? Madam would attempt a journey of this kind only if it were absolutely necessary and in supreme conformity with the will of God."

That gave Joe pause. After a moment, he said, "And Claire, you think it is? God's will, I mean?"

"I'm sure of it. This task has been given to Hannah and me to complete in the best way we can."

"Then I have no choice but to support you. Boy, how I wish I knew how to fly." He hugged me and held me tight. "I'll pray for you. I'll ask Regina and the folks to do the same."

"Thanks, sweetie." I broke the embrace and squeezed his hand. "Everything will work out."

"There's one condition."

"Yes?"

"I want to meet Laurence and Hannah before you go."

"Funny you should mention it. They'll be here tomorrow morning about six."

"Then let's have an early night. It's almost ten now."

"Perfect, I'm exhausted and I need to pack."

"I'll help. You'll need a sweater and a coat."

We started trudging up the stairs, our arms around each other.

"You have been reading about the South West area?" I said. "You knew it was cold?"

"For people who grew up in colder places, where constant warmth would feel unnatural. Gloves wouldn't be a bad idea, either. We'll make a list."

I laughed. How so like Joe to make a list, to focus on packing and preparing for a journey.

"We'll put prayer at the top and end of that list." I said and started pulling warm clothes out of a bottom drawer.

CHAPTER TWENTY-THREE

I opened one eye. Sunlight peeped in around the edges of our black-out curtains.

Sun! I shot up. "Cloud, what time is it?"

An espresso materialized on my bedside table.

"7:45, Madam. Joe said to let you sleep."

I looked at the bed. "Where's Joe?"

"Downstairs, with Laurence."

I threw the fluffy coverlet off, wrapped my ivory robe around my waist and clicked my ankle wings on. I got to our living room in two seconds. Paused. The study door was closed.

Taking a few breaths, I slowly walked to the door. I hesitated before knocking. I heard Laurence loudly concluding a story and then delivering a punch line. A moment of silence and then loud laughter. I knocked.

"Come in." Joe said.

They were seated side-by-side on the sofa, a large book in their laps. It all looked . . . comforting.

"Good morning, Claire." Laurence said.

"Yes, darling." Joe said. "Top of the morning, coffee?"

Maybe the 'darling' was a little proprietary. But it could be worse. "Uh, yes, please."

"Cloud, let's all have a round of lattes," Joe said.

The steaming drinks arrived. We sipped them in silence.

"So . . . you've met?"

The two men laughed.

"Laurence has been telling me the truth behind the myths about Lee's Lost Orders."

"Oh?"

"And I've promised to share with him all I know about Watergate."

"I've always pestered you about that story, Claire." Laurence said and slowly closed the book.

I sipped and nodded. "Where's Hannah?"

"Asleep in the living room with your dog," Laurence said. "Joe and I wanted to get to know each other, and she was still so sleepy. No need to wake her until we're ready. And you'll find her quite easily, just follow that dreadful perfume scent."

"As much as I hate to say this, I think we should leave." I said as I stood and rolled my shoulders up, down and back. "I'm ready whenever you are."

Laurence and Joe stood up.

"Right. Joe, I'm so glad we've had a chance to talk. It means a great deal to me."

They shook hands.

"And to me. I know anyone who cares as much as you do about getting old battlefield rumors clarified at 5:30 in the morning will take care of Claire and Hannah."

"And please don't worry. We'll be home within 48 hours or so."

Twenty minutes later, a still sleepy Hannah, Laurence and I were on a bus headed south.

"Why did you tell Joe 48 hours?"

Laurence looked straight ahead, as if his mind were elsewhere. "I've been doing some research. We must limit our time at our destination. It's not a safe place, especially for Hannah."

I nodded, turned and caught a last look at Beulah, just as our bus broke through a cirrostratus cloud and veered a sharp left. We were headed to the southern most reaches of Heaven.

CHAPTER TWENTY-FOUR

We took an express, so there was no planned stop between Beulah and the South East Gate. Most of our fellow passengers were dressed for a trip to Earth, which is typically taken from the southeastern portal.

Some had on Earth clothing, but most were fairly casual in flying jumpsuits. They checked their daypacks before leaving the bus to make sure they still had a map and any other necessary items.

Hannah had been sleeping off and on with her curly head lolling on my shoulder. But when the bus stopped, she jerked away.

"Where are we?" she said.

"One stop before the South East Gate, time to get off," Laurence said. "I asked the driver as a special favor to let us off early."

We hopped off at our cloud stop. From our vantage point, we could see the magnificent golden and pearl gate shining in the distance. We also found ourselves facing the primary stopping off destination for many Earth-bound angels—Pancho's. A low-slung ranch house near the gate, with a green and purple neon sign blinking out the ranch name, was about thirty yards away. We could see angels coming and going, some resting on the wrap-around-porch's rocking chairs, while others were sitting on picnic tables scattered around the front yard.

Cow-angels in boots, jeans, flannel shirts and hats moved from table to table, answering questions about various earth routes and offering food and drink.

"It's tempting." I said. "The chili is really good here."

"No time, Claire," Laurence said. "We have about four hours until dark. I have apples, let's start munching."

We sat for about five minutes on a cloud, eating our apples and watching the comings and goings as hundreds of angels streamed in and out of the huge gate. Laurence always asked a friend of his to bring back a bag of apples when his earth travels took him to New Zealand.

"Delicious." I said. "Thanks so much, Laurence."

"Where should I put the core?" Hannah said.

"Cloud, please dispose of our apple cores." Laurence said.

They vanished out of our hands.

"Thanks, Cloud. Let's get moving, friends." Laurence said.

"Which way?" Hannah said.

"See the dark clouds forming over there?" he said.

"Um . . . wow," Hannah said. "I've never seen black clouds like that. They look strange."

Laurence and I exchanged a quick look. "That's because you aren't familiar with storm clouds, young lady. So consider this an educational experience." he said.

"It may be educational, but it's definitely going to be cold." I said. "Let's put on our coats and gloves."

We zipped up our down, water repellent parkas. Hannah pulled on some pink mittens. Laurence and I were a bit more drab in navy and black gloves.

"Cool mittens, Hannah!" I said.

"Marie gave them to me."

"Really, when did you see her?"

"Last night. She heard we were going on a trip down south. Laurence told her I needed some gloves, and she got her cloud to send them to me."

"After this is over, we owe Marie a great dinner," Laurence said.

"She's always been a good friend."

"Oh, and she sent this pink ribbon to hold a small perfume bottle." Hannah said and waved the disgusting odor in our faces. "Isn't this cool? It's like a perfume necklace!"

"Hmmm." I said as I moved my face back from the tiny bottle. "Rethinking that dinner."

Laurence shook his head.

"Everybody ready?" Laurence squatted down low. "Up on my shoulders, Hannah."

"Really?"

Laurence seemed a bit exasperated. "Sure. Just hop up."

"Here, Hannah, let me give you a hand." I said and helped steady her as she swung one leg around Laurence's broad shoulders. She put her hands on the back of his neck.

"That's good. Grip the base of my neck. Just don't grab my throat. If you do, we may take a tumble."

"Let's go!" I said and headed west toward an increasingly darkening sky.

CHAPTER TWENTY-FIVE

We flew on silently through air that grew steadily colder. After an hour, ice clouds dripped around us as Laurence adeptly maneuvered through them. Then the sleet started.

"What's happening?" Hannah said.

Laurence and I slowed down so we could talk.

"It's sleet, sweetie," I said. "Frozen rain. It's okay, it won't hurt us."

"Did you bring your goggles?" Laurence asked.

"Joe packed them last night." God bless him and his lists.

"Let's get them out. I borrowed a smaller pair for Hannah."

We pulled ours on and showed Hannah how to wear hers. Better, but still not the greatest conditions for flying.

"What about our wings?" I said.

"We should have put a special wax on them." Laurence said. "But we didn't so I'm going to brush yours off and you do the same for me."

While Laurence hovered, I tried to pull and then brush off the little icicles that were forming on his wings. Then it was his turn to help me.

"Could we stop on that cloud over there?" I said. "I'm really tired. It's so much harder flying with soggy wings."

"No! That's an ice cloud. That would be a disaster. We've got to push on."

"How much longer?" Hannah said.

"We've been making good time," Laurence said. I'd say we're within an hour of the monastery."

"Have you seen any signs?" I said.

"No, but I'm using my compass and we're on the right course. Let's go."

He and Hannah swooped up over a frozen cloud. I followed as fast as I could.

The sleet stopped for about five minutes. I felt myself more relaxed with my flying. Then hail the size of golf balls slammed down on us.

"Quick! We've got to go faster." Laurence picked up the pace. His wings were so much bigger than mine, I was having a difficult time staying with them. I kept my eyes on Hannah's pink mittens, nearly all I could see through the gloom.

We climbed over another gigantic ice cloud. Then Laurence stopped abruptly. We were surrounded by a dark sky lit with thousands of twinkling stars.

"Look!" he said. "It's the diamond sky! Down there. I see it! We made it!"

Hannah and I peered down.

Floating like a mirage on a snow-covered cloud was a stone monastery with a tall wooden cross rising from the top of its highest peak. The grounds were illuminated by hundreds of torches stuck in the snow banks and along the building's walls. The brilliant stars that encircled the mission were brighter than any I had ever seen on Earth or in Heaven.

We could see a giant, bearded angel waving to us. The falling tiny ice crystals mixed with snowflakes didn't seem to faze him.

We dropped down into the wet snow. My wings were so soggy – I don't see how I could have flown any farther. Laurence's bedraggled wings swept the ground, looking as if they had been pelted with rocks and ice chunks for days. His down parka was soaked and clinging to his frame.

Hannah clapped her mittens together to knock off the ice. She pushed her hood down and looked up at the angel, who towered over all of us. His red beard and droopy mustache framed a big smile.

"Welcome! Welcome, brother and sisters!" he said with a little bow. "We are honored you have journeyed here. Please come inside and get your wet clothes off."

We saw *Locus Iste A Deo Factus Est* carved above the stone entry. This was the place.

He led us through a stone foyer into a large living and kitchen area. Each space had a walk-in fireplace, both of them blazing with the sparks and popping of newly laid fires.

"Please, my name is Columba, and you are most welcome. Perhaps you would like to see your rooms where you can change to dry clothes?"

"I'm not sure our clothes in our packs are dry," I said. "We flew through quite a bit of sleet and hail."

"Not to worry. Brigid and I have laid out simple clothing for you. Much as I have on." He pointed to his monk's habit and belt rope. I noticed he wore a pair of beautiful rose-colored sandals.

When I saw the room Hannah and I were to share, I wished I could stay a week. Its own large fireplace was roaring, and we sank into our beds as we sat on them to change out of our wet shoes.

"If I lie down now, I won't get up," I said. "Let's get dressed. Aren't you hungry? I am."

"I could eat a horse."

"Hannah, where in Heaven did you hear that expression?"

"Laurence said it the other night to Cloud, and Cloud said, 'I rather hope not, Master Laurence.'"

"Cloud – he's great. I miss him."

"Don't you and . . . Joe, is it? . . . have a cloud?"

"Of course. It's just that yours is very special. Ready? Let's go down."

The long wooden dining room table had been set with gleaming red pottery and silver cutlery. Three angels, all dressed in simple monk's garb, and all decidedly smaller than our greeter angel, were coming and going from the kitchen, setting dishes of food and hot bread on the table, bringing in bottles of wine and ale, arranging a centerpiece of yellow buttercups – all the while laughing and introducing themselves.

"Hello, I'm Aidan and this is Cuthbert."

"How do you do, I'm Claire and this is Hannah."

"A cupid!" Aidan said. "We rarely have cupids here. In fact, you're our second cupid guest in all these hundreds of years!"

"Wow!" said Hannah.

"Hannah, I'm Brigid. Don't suppose you drink ale. Would you like an apple cider?"

"Oh, yes, please."

Laurence came down the stairs, stooping a bit so as not to hit his head.

"This must be Laurence," said Cuthbert. "Meet Aidan and Brigid."

The big red-headed angel brought in wood from outside and carefully placed it on the nearest fire.

"And you've all met Columba. He is completely impervious to the elements and thus likes to meet and greet."

"I believe we're ready, shall we join hands?" Aidan said.

I took Hannah's hand and placed my other one in Columba's massive paw, where it nearly disappeared. But his grip was gentle and warm.

Aidan turned his eyes upward. "Our Father, we thank you for our guests. We know their visit with us is not a casual one and we thank you for trusting them into our care. Help us to guide them, and to be with them in spirit through their task. In nomine Patris et Filii et Spiritus Sancti. Amen."

We all simultaneously crossed ourselves and said "Amen."

We sat down in silence.

Laurence spoke first. "Thank you for your kind and loving hospitality. Our journey was difficult and it is good to be with friends."

"It is we who are honored." Aidan said. "As I told you we've hosted only one other cupid who was completing a twelfth-year assignment." He stood and began filling our wine and ale glasses according to our wishes.

"And that more than one hundred years ago." Cuthbert said and began passing the warm, brown bread. "His Twelfth Year Mission was the strenuous task of flying here and back — well, from the South East Gate to here and back again. Alone. With only a three-hour stop here. It was quite an accomplishment."

"Yes, that's very impressive." I said, remembering my sodden wings.

"But we noticed Hannah didn't fly here." Brigid said.

Hannah looked down. I nearly jumped in, but I thought she should answer for herself.

Hannah looked up and attempted a weak smile. "About a week ago, my right wing was stolen."

Our hosts all looked at each other and nodded quietly.

"The Great Gabriel began working with Claire," she said, "and in a way, with me — and we started getting messages, clues to help in the search. The last one led us here."

No one spoke. Brigid and Columba began passing a platter of roasted chicken, squash, okra, and green beans. I was already feeling full after the fresh sourdough bread.

"Gabriel was here two nights ago." Columba said. "His was a brief stay, but he told us to expect you and what would be expected of us in return."

"Good," Laurence said. "So glad he's briefed you."

"Gabriel shared . . . what he felt was necessary." Aidan said. "There's always some work left for us to do, after all. May we see the last message so as to understand better why you are here?"

"Of course." I said. "Hannah?"

First, Hannah slipped out the perfumed necklace that had been tucked into her outer sweater. Our four hosts' eyes met. Then she reached farther under her sweater and pulled out the message from her blouse pocket.

"Please, read and share," she said as she handed the note to Aidan.

Aidan read silently. Then he coughed lightly.

"I'll pass this around to each of you, to see if something lies beneath the surface. But let me read it out loud first."

"This Place was made by God

And yet it's very near to Evil.

Take the key to its neighbor, but be wary.

Dress warmly, sing together, and don't tarry."

No one spoke. Laurence cut into his chicken and Columba did the same.

Finally, Cuthbert broke the silence. "Let us reflect on this for a few minutes. Since in many ways we still lead a monastic life, we often find it beneficial to dine in silence, allowing God and the Holy Spirit to nourish our minds, our creativity as well as our bodies. I suggest we do this now. We can gather for dessert and coffee in the living room. I believe by then we'll be prepared to interpret this message and indeed to offer advice."

"Thank you, Cuthbert." I said.

The next thirty minutes were filled only by a ticking clock in the kitchen. When Aidan saw that everyone had eaten what he or she wanted, he stood.

"Juniper, our brother who left this morning to travel on a Corporate assignment, knew you were coming and arose early to bake one of his delicious apple pies. Let us move to more comfortable seating and enjoy our dessert and coffee."

We quickly settled in with enormous helpings of pie. It seemed Juniper baked two, so Brigid was very generous in her portions. I helped Columba make and serve coffee. Aidan, Cuthbert and Laurence sat together in a corner, looking at the message. The two monks seemed to be in agreement on a point that Laurence was not buying.

"Aidan, why don't you and Cuthbert discuss this with the rest?" Laurence said. "You know my opinion."

"We shall, only because we are commanded by God to do so," Aidan said. "Would that we had any other news for you."

Oh dear. This sounded bad.

CHAPTER TWENTY-SIX

Brigid picked up her own coffee and pie and took the seat next to Hannah. "So far, you have been on this quest with Claire?"

Hannah nodded.

"We needed Laurence to help us get Hannah here." I said.

"Yes." Cuthbert said. "That was wise. But Laurence will not be going on the final journey."

"Wait," Hannah said, "I thought we were here. How much farther are we going?"

"I'm afraid you must go to our evil neighbor." Columba said.

I felt sick.

"You know I think that can't be right," Laurence said.

"It's the only way to make sense of the message," Aidan said.

We three travelers looked at each other. Hannah snuggled closer to me. She seemed a bit shaky.

"Is that even possible?" Laurence said. "I mean, I know it's possible, but does one enter and get out safely? And a cupid? There must be another interpretation."

"Read the message again." Brigid said. "You are here in a place made by God and we are near Evil. You are to visit our neighbor. Our nearest neighbor controls the South West Gate."

Then it seemed as if everyone started talking at once. Hannah looked as if she were going to cry. I put my arm around her. Laurence's voice got louder.

"Silence!" said Aidan. "Please, we do not believe God has asked this cupid to do a task she cannot do. In fact, please center yourselves by taking deep breaths and consider the tools she's been given."

All of us were quiet for a few moments. Then Cuthbert spoke.

"We aren't dismissing the dangers of the journey. We may know them better than any of you. But remember Gabriel asked us to assist you. Please tell us about any object that has been given to you since you began your search for the wing."

I looked at Hannah. She blew her nose.

"Hannah, who starts, me or you?"

She moved out from under my arm and straightened her back. Good girl.

"I will. The first place we visited was backstage at the Heavenly Host. I got an earful. Well, two earfuls."

"An earful." said Columba. "I've heard of such a thing, but never had one. Never heard one either."

"Brigid has," Cuthbert said.

Brigid was beaming. "When I first came to Heaven. Before I moved here. After I went through orientation, I was assigned to help with Awakenings. There weren't so many people on Earth as there are now, and it seems like we took longer preparing the family members who were going to receive their loved one. Sometimes we worked with the Heavenly Host – Caedmon was their director then – who would give a family member an earful.

"Then later that day or even during that first week, whenever the family wanted to share the song, they did. It was just a magnificent gift for the family and the newcomer."

"Yes, I can see that." I said.

"Claire's husband recently came through." Laurence said.

"Oh, that reminds me, I really need to get a message back to Joe, to let him know we've arrived safely. Could we ask your cloud?"

Brigid, Cuthbert, Aidan and Columba looked at each other. At first, no one spoke.

"I'm sorry, I didn't mean to be rude. Perhaps you don't use your cloud the way we do in the other parts of Heaven. Everything is more, oh, old-fashioned here." I immediately regretted saying this.

"Did you not see the chimneys?" Columba said. "At least we don't have to deal with fire pits and smoke holes."

Brigid shot him a warning glance.

"No, no, it's not that, dear." she said.

"Let us be completely open and honest with you." Aidan said.

"Please." said Laurence.

"This is an outpost." said Aidan. "Few people visit here in say, twelve months time. Therefore, any time we get visitors, this is noted by the guards of the South West Gate."

"They know we're here?" I said.

"They know we have visitors. They don't know whom or why. Our stone walls are thick with hundreds of years of prayers and praise. Evil cannot penetrate.

"However, if our cloud carries a message, this can be intercepted. Not it can be, it would be. This would be incredibly useful information that could easily undermine your task. It's simply not worth it. I hope you understand."

"Yes, of course. Joe will be okay. Laurence told him we'd be back in about two days." I was disappointed, but what could I do?

"That sounds about right." Columba said.

"Dear ones, back to the earfuls." said Brigid.

"Oh, yes." said Hannah.

"This is the most important thing. I assume you were given songs you know by heart?"

We nodded.

"Well, I had to learn the last verse of one, but I'm good." said Hannah.

"As the bearer of the earful, you must begin the song."

Hannah nodded.

"And you must not stop singing until the Host stop singing."

"Okay."

"Claire, if you join in, the same rule applies to you. You must not stop singing until the heavenly chorus finishes its song."

"Got it."

"What else were you given?"

"A key." Hannah said.

"A key to what?" Aidan said.

"To the first home a Castle resident was given." Hannah said.

"Could we see it?" Cuthbert said.

Hannah pulled out her pink velveteen necklace again. For the first time, I noticed the platinum and diamond key was hanging with the tiny perfume bottle.

Cuthbert passed the key around and then returned it to Hannah.

"This key will open something else, something very important," he said.

"Maybe the South West Gate?"

Our hosts shook their heads.

"No, no, there's no need for a key there." Aidan said. "We would never lock it, in case some poor tortured soul wishes to escape. And the gates are always opened for any poor fool from Heaven who passes by, perhaps accidentally, perhaps not."

"But why?" said Hannah.

"To turn him or her to the Wicked Way." Brigid said. "And from the Wicked Way, the path back to God is difficult and steep."

"But not impossible," Cuthbert said. "That's why we're here, to go forth and fight for any who wish to come back."

Columba was wearing a slight grin. "We Celtic monks, you know, we're used to being a lone outpost in the midst of darkness. Feels like home to us."

"So, if the gate is never locked," Laurence said, "why is there a gate at all?"

Laurence sipped his coffee. "No more so than any of us, but you knew that."

I put my coffee down. "Laurence, I didn't sleep much last night. I think it's the fear of the unknown. I mean, is this going to be a horror show? Are we going to be thrown things that twist Hannah's spirit forever?"

"I wish I knew."

"We should have gone to morning prayer."

"I'll bet you prayed most of the night."

"Yes, of course. You, too."

"Probably our little cherub at well."

"I know she's uneasy, but I'm not sure she's really frightened."

"All to Columba's point."

I got up and stretched. I peeked outside and it was still gray. No sign of light yet. "Where are you going?" he said.

"Gotta try on these boots and other gear. Then wake up Hannah so we can at least eat breakfast. Don't know how long we'll be gone."

"Columba said something about oatmeal. Hope that's okay."

"Comfort food that sticks to your ribs? It's perfect. See you in a bit."

When I was dressed, I woke up Hannah and helped her put on her wool undies and boots. We decided to put our new gloves in our parka pockets.

The breakfast table was beautifully laid out with silver cutlery and huge purple pottery bowls. Oatmeal steamed from them and a large pot of honey and pitcher of cream stood in the center.

We filled our bowls and took our seats. This wasn't a silent meal. In fact, it seemed the monks were brighter than usual to distract us from what was coming.

Cuthbert told Hannah how he used to be a shepherd.

"Ah, yes, in the Lammermuir hills. One night, I was dozing off with my sheep all around me. I looked up and saw bright lights held by angels who were passing up a huge staircase in the sky. The stairs stretched all the way from Earth into the heavens."

Hannah nodded for him to go on. I realized that this was old school for her – angels with lights traveling up to heaven was part of her everyday life. Her world view was so radically different! Would she be safe today? I had to have faith that she would be.

"The next day, I learned that during the night—at the exact time of my vision – our dedicated apostolate, Aidan, who had served our community for about 16 years, had died. God had allowed me to see beautiful angels bringing his soul home. This inspired me with wonder. I decided to study hard and pursue a life dedicated to Christ."

"That's a lovely story, Cuthbert." I said.

"I didn't get to see angels until I became one." said Laurence. Everyone laughed.

"Light is here." Brigid said. "It typically stays light for two to three hours. So. . ."

"So, we must go." I said. "Ready, Hannah?"

Laurence hugged us. The others wished us "Godspeed and a safe return!"

Columba went outside with us. We stood in the morning mists, watching a snow cloud form. Columba pointed to a cloud and we watched it swirl away to reveal a black form.

"Hannah, see the two black ice fences over there to the west? That's where you must go. Quickly. Don't knock on the gate. Open it and enter as far as you can before you are noticed. Perhaps you'll see the wing immediately. We have no way of knowing."

Hannah and I nodded.

"Yes, thank you, Columba. I understand." she said.

"And, Clarie? I don't know why you've been chosen to accompany Hannah on this, but as my dear friend Jack once wrote: 'Our Lord does all things for each.' So . . . stay open to possibilities."

"I . . . yes, thank you."

Columba hugged us. "Now climb on Claire's shoulders and go!"

We were at the tall ice-covered gate within an hour. Hannah

pushed on it, but it didn't budge. I leaned into it and it creaked a bit.

Both of us stepped back and rammed it together with our shoulders. It swung open. We stepped through and the gate slammed behind us.

It was completely black inside. Cold vapors hit our exposed faces. Hannah clung to me. I tried to catch my breath.

Then a female voice roared, "Let there be light!"

CHAPTER TWENTY-EIGHT

Boom! Boom! Boom! Vast caverns were instantly illuminated all around us. We were on a hill looking down on a scene reminiscent of Earth's vast underground caves, like Carlsbad or Blanchard Springs. But there were no vivid colors, only tall, dark shadows made by ice stalagmites and stalactites. Legions of bats hung from icicles dripping from the cathedral-like ceiling.

Then a high-pitched giggle echoed in the darkness. "I've always wanted to say that."

We looked in the direction of the woman. She was clothed in a pink-feathered coat with a hood. Her white wheelchair was perched on the edge of another hill across from us.

She waved. It was . . . not what either of us had expected. Then she pushed her wheels and rolled down the incline.

"Wheeeeeeeeee!"

She skidded to a stop on a ledge just below us.

"So much fun, now you try," she shouted up to us.

Hannah looked at me. I hesitated.

"C'mon, c'mon, this won't be any fun at all if you don't join me. I know where your wing is, so come on down!"

Slowly I stepped out on the ice and motioned for Hannah to follow.

The person in the chair twisted her face up to us. Her neck moved in unnatural ways, a bit like an owl. "That's it, and if you fall, mama will be here to catch you."

We looked at each other. Hannah nodded. We took step by step and slowly we could see that the boots were going to hold on the ice. With each step we were bolder, and soon we were half-way down the hill.

"Not fair! Where did you get those boots? Don't answer, I can guess."

She drummed her white-gloved fingers impatiently on the chair's arms. After about three more minutes, we stood before her.

She pulled back her hood to reveal long, shining black hair. Leaning over, she shook it as if to give it more shape. Then she pushed herself up from the chair and took a step toward us. We stepped back.

"You didn't think I really needed the chair, did you, darlings? Just like to make an entrance."

Now that we were close to her, we could see that her face was pale, almost translucent. Veins ran in a crazy patchwork pattern that covered her face and neck like a red and blue web.

She kicked the chair and it tumbled down into a valley, echoing and clattering as it went down.

"Claire, so pleased you're here. I'm Angelica, a delegate of . . . well, you know who. What may I do for you?"

"For me, nothing."

"Ah. The little one, then."

Hannah moved a bit closer to me. "I want my wing back." She said in a small voice.

Angelica held out her arm and pressed her palm toward Hannah. "Please don't get any closer with that wretched scent. Besides, I don't like cupids."

I quickly considered this. "That means you're stronger than me down here, Hannah. She's afraid of you or she wouldn't have said that."

As Angelica laughed, the veins in her neck and face began to bulge. "Afraid of a cupid?"

"Where is my wing?" Hannah's voice was a bit bolder.

When she didn't answer, Hannah took a step toward her.

She backed away and answered with a hiss. "Listen, sister, I said stay away from me."

Quickly, as if she knew all along she would do this, Hannah began to sing.

"Holy, holy, holy, Lord God Almighty!

Early in the morning our song shall rise to Thee."

Then in full and awesome unison, the Heavenly Host joined in. It was as if they were all around us. Their triumphant harmonies echoed back and forth across the chambers.

"Holy, Holy, Holy! Merciful and Mighty!

God in Three Persons, blessed Trinity!"

As the horns joined in and the strings surged upward, the evil woman stepped back and shivered.

Hannah and the Host continued. Hannah stood straighter and with each line moved along the ledge as if she knew where to go. She turned and took my hand. It seemed as if our boots were forcefully leading us toward an open doorway.

"Holy, Holy, Holy, all the saints adore Thee,

Casting down their golden crowns around the glassy sea;

Cherubim and Seraphim falling down before Thee,

Which wert, and art, and evermore shalt be."

Angelica was squatting on the ground, softly moaning and holding her ears with her hands. Hannah pulled me into a small room. Its lights came on as we stepped inside.

There, on the wall, mounted inside a frost-covered case, was a small wing.

"My wing!"

The timpani were cuing up for a final drum roll. Then suddenly, the music stopped.

"No, don't stop. Keep singing!"

But the Heavenly Host had finished. Silence.

Uh-oh.

I stared up at the wing in its case, the reason we were there. It seemed so close, so accessible. But standing up to retrieve it took more energy than I would ever have.

"I think I really must be going now," Angelica said. "I have more bad people to welcome and more awful things to do."

She turned and slammed the little room's door shut. All the lights went out.

We sat there in the dark for a few minutes. I stopped crying, but now Hannah was sobbing. I felt like putting my head in her lap and just sleeping for a while. It was so bitterly cold. It would feel so good to go to sleep.

"Claire, can you hate someone in Heaven?"

Through my foggy brain, I recognized that Hannah had asked a question. I had to try to answer.

"No, no, I . . . don't think so. Why?" I reached for her face through the darkness. My gloves found her and I wiped the tears from her eyes and face.

"Because I hate my dad."

I had never heard hardness in her voice before. It shocked me out of myself for a moment. "What–Laurence, no, you–"

"No, my Earth dad."

"You never knew him."

"The night of the accident, when Michael scooped me up in his arms and flew me to the top of a tree, we looked down, and my dad was calling out for my mom. I listened but he never called my name."

"What? Oh, honey, people on Earth, when something like an accident happens, people go into a thing called shock. It messes up your mind so you can't think. In fact, it's . . . I'm feeling now." Some clarity began to impose itself again, just a hint of light. "We've got to get up and moving. We can't sit here or we'll never get up."

"Shock? Are you sure? Do you think he called out for me after Michael carried me away? So I shouldn't hate him?"

"No, you shouldn't hate him. I'm sure he's thought of you every day since. I'm very sure of it. And some day, he can tell you so himself. Now help me get up."

But Hannah stayed crouched on the bottom step. "Who's Jamie?"

"My son. He was very, very sick on Earth. God brought him to Heaven after a while, but he was very sick while he was on Earth, so Joe and I were sad a lot."

"So many things to learn. But I don't want to hate my dad anymore."

A bitterly icy wind blew in suddenly, almost breaking down the door. The room temperature seemed to drop twenty degrees, sapping our strength. This was getting dangerous. I needed to focus on the present.

"Yes, listen, we have to find a way out of here."

"But I have to get my wing. Oh, look, over there!"

I lifted my head. The tips of the wing were glowing. I could see Hannah's face again.

She looked at me. "Claire, you always told me that you were in Heaven because you believed. Is that true?"

I exhaled slowly. "Yes, that and by God's grace."

"Then let's sing."

I squeezed her hand. "You start. But we can't stop."

"Are you washed in the blood?" Her voice was faint, trembly. "In the soul-cleansing blood of the Lamb?"

I joined in as strongly as I could, pushing back my tears with my gloved hands.

"Are your garments spotless? Are they white as snow?"

Then the soprano and alto Hosts chimed in. "Are you washed in the blood of the Lamb?"

The tempo picked up and the rhythm strengthened as we held hands and climbed the stairs together. The wing was brighter now.

"Have you been to Jesus for the cleansing pow'r?

Are you washed in the blood of the Lamb?

Are you fully trusting in His grace this hour?

Are you washed in the blood of the Lamb?"

Then a gorgeous rippling of chords marked a key change, and another burst of the Host, this time with the full complement of bass and tenors. This was a cappella, and the resounding harmonies seemed to melt the icy chamber.

I didn't feel sick anymore. I could feel life returning to my feet and hands. The little wing was fully lit, from top to bottom, root to tips. Moving my mouth to sing was resuscitating my face.

"Are you washed in the blood,

In the soul-cleansing blood of the Lamb?"

Hannah pulled the key from around her neck and slipped it in the lock. We held our breaths.

The case popped open.

I reached up and my gloves gripped the wing and helped me pull it down. I fitted it on Hannah's back, all the while both of us were singing as loudly as we could manage. Hannah pulled the key out.

"Let's go," I said and tapped my heart. She did the same and we lifted off. We stopped and hovered in front of the chamber's door and watched it quickly open. We zipped over Angelica as she was making her way along the ice bridge.

She sank down as we passed. "No!" Her cry ricocheted around the cave.

We flew through the main cave toward the gate. Hannah held out her gloved fingers, and the gate surged twice against its locks, then burst open. Up and out into the frigid dark. We finished the song as we eagerly made our way to the monastery. I looked at Hannah and saw that her wing, now that we no longer needed its light, appeared normal.

"Are your garments spotless? Are they white as snow?

Are you washed in the blood of the Lamb?"

The mission's torches were twinkling around the tall cross. The diamond sky had never looked more beautiful. Columba was waving us down. We settled and fell into his arms.

Everyone hugged us and Laurence put us into a big feather bed where we slept most soundly.

CHAPTER TWENTY-NINE

After breakfast the next morning, Laurence, Hannah and I gathered our belongings downstairs, prepared to leave.

"Hannah, let me see your wings, please." Cuthbert said.

Hannah popped her wings out. Everyone spontaneously formed a little circle around her and clapped.

"This has been a hard journey for you." Aidan said. "But you have proved your mettle and your faith.

"Claire shared the story of her oldest child, her feeble son—I know in the 20th and 21st Century you called such children 'disabled'—and we should have known someone from the Wicked Way would try to use that against her. And your father's confusion and state of shock after his car accident is something you could have never understood on your own."

"Aidan, the wing has been there for some time now." Brigid said. Her voice showed concern.

Aidan's hands ran over Hannah's wing. He felt the top and smoothed the feathers with his fingers.

"Yes, I see." he said. "Hannah, this wing still holds the mark of evil. Allow us to anoint it with healing oil."

Hannah looked at Laurence and me.

"Yes, of course." Laurence said. "It must be contaminated."

"But probably not as much as you might think." Columba said. "Knowing what we know of our enemy, we suspect they did not plan on acquiring a cupid's wing—the ultimate source of innocence."

CHAPTER THIRTY

I arrived exhausted, and Joe sent me straight to bed without even a question, God bless him. Now he was joining me for breakfast after my long sleep.

I knew how much he wanted to hear about the adventure and had decided to start with the most difficult parts, to get them out of the way.

"Joe, Jamie came up after we entered the South West Gate."

He put his hot chocolate down and turned to me. "After you . . . What in heaven's name do you mean?"

"That's just it, we were not technically in Heaven. It was a sort of strange evil place that Brigid called the Wicked Way. A way that led to the darker depths of Hell — of that, I'm sure."

He put his arms around me and held me for a moment. "What happened?"

"There was this disgustingly awful woman, very pale and ugly, who greeted us and locked us in the room where the wing was mounted on the wall."

"Laurence said something about using the key the Castle resident gave you. We talked a bit after you had gone up to bed. Hannah played with Rosie while he caught me up."

"Well, I . . . fell apart when she mentioned Jamie's name."

Joe sighed. This was familiar ground. "Claire, he lived with us for fourteen years. Fourteen years you took care of him almost every day. Nights I was on duty. We hardly had any lives we could call our own. We neglected Sarah and William. Your parents practically raised them until they started school."

"I know, I know."

"We loved him, but we needed to start giving that time to our other family. We've been over this so many times. And you said Jamie is whole and well here."

"He looks good, very good."

Joe put his arms around me again and we hugged for a long time.

"We have to move on," Joe said. "We're all living here. I want to see him."

"Sure, let's go tomorrow. Joe, would you consider living with Hannah and Laurence?" I'd decided to just go for it. No use tap-dancing around this.

Joe put his book down. "You miss them terribly, don't you?"

"Yes, especially Hannah. I thought about bringing her over here, but I think she's had too much disruption in her life during the past couple of weeks."

"I would . . . consider it."

"Oh, Joe, that would be terrific."

"Where would we live?"

"I thought we might go talk to them and perhaps that would sort itself out."

"Okay, let's go."

I laughed. "We don't have to go this very minute. For one thing, I need to teach you how to fly."

He was pulling on his clothes. "Maybe."

"What? Don't tell me—Regina."

"Of course, my big sis wasn't going to just feed me, she had to teach me a new trick, too. I like it, let's go so I can show you."

I threw off the covers. "Okay, you've convinced me. Give me a few moments to get dressed."

Joe was already out the door. Soon he was hovering outside the bedroom window!

Good grief. "Coming!"

"Oh, it is locked sometimes," Brigid said. "From the inside. Particularly after an escape. There hasn't been one lately."

I was barely listening to the exchange. I was still . . . was I expected to take an innocent cupid literally through the gates of Hell?

"Do you have any other tools to use tomorrow?" said Cuthbert.

"I can't think of any." Hannah said and looked at me. I was afraid she was correct. It seemed like a pitifully small arsenal.

"Don't worry, child." Brigid said. "We have some gifts. First, the cold you will encounter tomorrow is so frigid it may seem hot. We have undergarments for you to put on tonight and wear tomorrow. They're made of the finest spun silver and gold wool and yet very light. We all wear them, especially if we're outside or closer to the South West Gate."

"And we have special boots for the ladies," Columba said. "Boots made of prayers sent up to heaven for hundreds of years. After God hears them, he lets us have them. The boots are incredibly warm and will allow you to go sure-footed on the slipperiest ice. They also will not let you take a wrong turn or wrong path. We'll place them outside your door tonight."

"You'll be wearing gloves made of new parents' laughter and tears." Aidan said. "The Archangel Vincent gathers them up on Earth and sends them to us on a regular basis. They will warm your hands and fingers and will show your hands what to do in any circumstance. They will be with your boots when you wake up tomorrow."

"All together, you'll be armed with boots and gloves of hope, ear-fuls of faith, and a key of love." said Brigid. "And while you are gone, we will all be in prayer for your safe return to us."

"With the wing on Hannah's back." Laurence said. "And how could you not bring it back after hearing about all these incredible gifts?"

Hannah smiled and grabbed my hand.

I smiled back. But I knew I wanted a good night's sleep. Morning would come too early.

CHAPTER TWENTY-SEVEN

Laurence was alone in the kitchen when I came down. We had been cautioned not to leave until daylight, and that wouldn't come until about eight. It was 6:30. Plenty of time to get Hannah up.

"Where is everyone?"

"At lauds. Started at six. I just didn't get up in time to make it."

"Ummm. Coffee?"

"Yes, it's still hot."

I grabbed a cup and filled it. I sat in front of Laurence.

"Claire, Columba and I talked for a while after everyone had gone to bed."

"And?"

"The weapons Hannah has been given are clearly powerful, but the strongest of all went unmentioned last night."

"What?"

"Hannah."

"I don't understand."

"Think about it. She doesn't really understand sin. Nor evil. In the abstract, perhaps, but she has no real experience with it."

"Doesn't that make her all the more vulnerable?"

"I asked him that and he didn't think so. He thought that's why you're along."

"So I'm the poster child for sin?"

"That's why it was mounted and locked away." said Cuthbert.

"Oh, I see." I hadn't thought that her wing could be dangerous to them.

"Hannah, please kneel, this won't hurt." Aidan said.

He placed his left hand on her right wing. Brigid held a small jar of oil for him. She poured a small amount into his right palm.

"This wing was made by God. It is inviolate and good." he said. "May it bear its owner through many happy skies, whether she be on Earth or in Heaven."

He rubbed the oil on the wing's tips.

"In nomine Patris et Filii et Spiritus Sancti, Amen."

We made the sign of the cross and repeated his amen.

"Now, rise, Hannah the Cupid!" said Aidan, "You have many miles to fly on your journey home."

Hannah stood up with a great air of solemnity.

Laurence broke the silence. "Thank you, Aidan. And thanks, Brigid and Cuthbert, for packing a lunch for us to eat on the bus."

Brigid hugged Hannah as we stood outside of the mission. Aidan, Columba, and Cuthbert did the same, then it was Laurence and my time for hugs and well wishes.

"May God bring you safely home." Cuthbert said. "Let it be a golden and peaceful day."

"Please visit us again," said Aidan. "Next time will be much more pleasant."

"Yes, Hannah, say you'll come and spend a week or so with us." Brigid said. "There's nothing we'd like better. It's been good to have a cupid here. Brightens the place up."

"I'll come back again." Hannah said. "I couldn't have done any of this without your help."

"And Claire's." Columba said.

Hannah reached up to my chest and touched my heart. "Without Claire, it would have been impossible."

I caught Columba's eye. "He does all things for each."

"That's been my experience," Columba said.

"Let it be a golden and peaceful day." Laurence said and then turned to us. "Okay, folks, let's go while there's still light!"

Laurence shot up and we followed his lead, turning to wave one last time as we headed to the South East Gate.

Our flying time there seemed to go very fast, much faster than the way in, and soon we boarded the express for Beulah.

"Joe's going to be so worried." I said.

"No, he's not." said Laurence.

"But I couldn't get word to him, and he expected to hear from me."

"He did. I flew over here after you two left and sent a message through Pancho's cloud. Cuthbert assured me it was out of reach of interference."

I smiled. "That was so thoughtful!"

"I knew I'd want to know if I had been left behind. And besides, it gave me something to do instead of sitting around at the mission and praying all day."

"They were sweet." Hannah said.

"Yes, but more than sweet." Laurence said. "They are very strong to endure that place. Very impressive. It's not for everyone."

"We were lucky they were there to help us." I said.

"And now I can't wait to get back to our part of Heaven."

We unpacked the sacks the monks had given us and ate crispy brown rolls and chunks of flaky goat cheese, deviled eggs, and crisp tart apples. There was also a goat skin of light ale. It was a perfect lunch for the bus ride back. Laurence said the deviled eggs were an especially nice touch.

"I mean, remember the time you and Joe visited, and you saw the mouse run across Jamie's room? I think that might have been right after the big, 'You're not changing my son's diapers often enough' scene. Such a fab place to live."

Hannah had walked up a few more steps, but now she turned back. "What's she talking about, Claire? Are you all right?"

"Something long time ago. Sorry."

Everything in that suddenly unbearably frigid place became distorted. I felt nausea sweeping over me. Next I started shaking and couldn't stop. Then the sobbing began. Years of pain and guilt that the happiness of Heaven had papered over, buried, but not abolished.

Hannah ran down the steps to me and started hugging me. "It's okay, Claire. I'm here. Don't let her get to you."

Angelica put her hands on her hips and blocked the doorway. "This is so sweet. Hannah, does this remind you of something? If only at the car wreck your father had held you like this, just like you're holding Claire."

Hannah released her hug and stood in silence, staring at Angelica. Her hands were balled into tight fists. Her sullen face and eyes had a flash of anger I had never seen.

"Oh, well, tell you what. Just stay here for a few years, maybe a decade or so and work it out. You'll be comfortable here. You'll feel like you belong."

I was still shaking. Hannah sank down beside me. Then she started beating her fists on her legs.

"Oh, Claire!" she cried. "I hate it here! I hate her!"

Angelica leaned forward and we looked up at her huge snarling mouth. "Of course, you do, you darling, adorable cupid. So does the angel with you. We bring out only the best in our guests. So, take an icy seat. Stay awhile. Cry to each other. I mean, really, you didn't think you were going anywhere, did you? You can look at the wing forever as far as we're concerned but you have no way to open the case. And the only way you could get out would be for both of you to fly out. So . . . sorry, sweeties."

"And just when I was starting to enjoy it." Angelica was leaning in the doorway. "Ah, yes, you found the little wing. Some friend of ours in Heaven happened upon it, and it does make such a nice trophy, n'est pas?"

Hannah pursed her lips together. "It's my wing! Somebody stole it!"

"Oh, dear, Claire, can't you do something? I'm afraid she's going to throw a bit of a tantrum."

"No, she's going to fight for what's hers. And this is not my battle."

She continued to lean against the doorway and was now filing her curled fingernails. "I say, Claire, since you seem so comfy in the mother role, how is Jamie these days?"

I caught my breath. My heart started racing. "What – what do you mean?"

Hannah looked up at me. "Who's Jamie?"

"Don't pay attention to her, she's just trying to divert you."

Angelica laughed. I had never heard so much contempt packed into a single sound.

"What a good mother you've become, all of a sudden. Such a pity Jamie never saw it. Or I suppose he sort of saw you, lying in that bed all those years. Desperately trying to lift up his head."

I sank down on one of the steps leading to the wing display. I waved Hannah away.

"Please go on." I said, gasping. "Your boots and gloves will help."

"This is so touching, people!" Angelica said with a screech and her arms extended upward. "Really, such an emotional display never seen on Heaven or on Earth or on the Way."

"What do you want?" I said.

"Why, I think that would be obvious. We want you, darling. You're such a great sinner. We've been waiting for you ever since you abandoned your first born to that horrid state institution."

I propped my forehead with my hands and looked down.

"I stand unaware of any definitive research on this topic, but let me ponder a brief while."

"Please do." Joe said. "I have a mild bet riding on it."

"Then by all means, sir, I shall manage to satisfy both parties, without rancor nor disappointment. After all, this is Heaven."

looked at Laurence. His normal caramel-colored complexion looked a bit peaked.

"I can answer that." he said.

"Okay."

"I've agreed to let Tiffany live here for one month while her angel-parents are on special assignment to Earth. I've been waiting for the right moment to tell you."

Joe, Marie, and I looked at each other and laughed.

"This seems like the right time." I said. "When does the month start?"

"Yesterday. She moved into your old room last night. I was advised that if I let them share a room, they would never get any sleep."

"So, we'll be parents to two cupids for a month, right?" Joe said.

"Correct." Laurence was very solemn and yet I could tell he wanted to laugh at the craziness of it all.

"Cloud." I said. "Please bring us champagne and flutes. Time to celebrate."

"Right away, Madam."

After two glasses of champagne, Marie left and the three of us sat together, staring at the fire. We heard Hannah and Tiffany running from one bedroom to another, then getting mysteriously quiet, then running again.

"Girls are easier than boys." Joe said.

"Nope, it's the other way around." I said.

"I'll bet you one breakfast in bed."

"That you'll do yourself, with only a wee bit of help from Cloud?"

"Or you, since you're going to lose."

Laurence held up his hands. "We need an expert opinion. Cloud, who is supposed to be easier to raise, girls or boys?"

"Are we discussing Earth children, Master Laurence, or cupids?"

"Cupids."

"His friend, Jack, is C.S. Lewis. He talked about how they had become great friends when Lewis made a pilgrimage to the monastery not long after his Awakening."

"Wow." said Marie. "Who else has visited them?"

"Not sure, but it was definitely one of the most fascinating places I've been to in the last, oh, one hundred years. Also, the most dangerous. Good to be home."

"Speaking of home. Isn't that why we're here?" Joe said.

Cloud was clearing his throat. Marie rolled her eyes.

Laurence spoke to Cloud first. "Yes, Cloud?"

"Master Laurence, if I may be so bold, I have taken certain liberties regarding the prospect of Madam Claire and Master Joe taking up residence here."

"Proceed."

"Yes, well, I have a blueprint showing a new wing upstairs that would include a bedroom for Master Joe and one for Madam Claire, with a rather attractive study adjoining the two rooms."

An architectural drawing appeared before us on the coffee table. We examined it for a few moments.

"I see, Cloud. Where would you propose Rosie, our dog, could stay?"

"Madam Claire, I have indicated her bed quite near to yours. I believe this is in keeping with your Earth arrangements."

I looked at Laurence. "Can you live with a dog? Rosie is usually quiet. Except when she isn't."

"To quote Cloud, all is serene here."

"That's terrific. Joe and I appreciate it. Joe, what do you think?"

"It looks good. Cloud, how long to build?"

"Approximately seven minutes." We all smiled.

Joe coughed to keep from laughing. "Okay, very good."

"Cloud, what will happen to my old room?" I asked.

Cloud began clearing his throat again. This was annoying. I

"Yep, that's what I think." Tiffany said and turned to Hannah. "We've got to finish our science fair homework so we can watch 'The Parent Trap.' Laurence promised."

"Oops, I forgot. May we be excused?"

They both stood up. Plates and glasses empty.

"By all means." Laurence said.

The two cupids walked toward Hannah's room.

"Science fair?" Joe mouthed.

"Don't ask." I said.

"Claire, one thing we've forgotten was Joe's homecoming." Laurence said.

"Ah, yes, I do seem to remember a strange event." Joe said.

"What happened?" Marie said.

"We were crouched down and covered by archangels for about five minutes while we were in the river. I was scared, but thought perhaps this was a common thing. I learned later it wasn't."

"Mercy!" Marie said. "This whole adventure seems to have touched all of us."

"Ummmmm," Joe said, "If I may interject as a newbie, it seems once this got rolling, all of us had some role to play, however small or big. We all were supporting Hannah and Claire – helping with clues, offering advice, praying, or just being there for them. We had to have faith–big time–to roll with all of this."

"As I heard just recently, He does all things for each."

I reached out my arms and gave Joe a hug. "I know it hasn't been easy on you, to come to your new home while all this has been going on."

Joe shrugged. "We seem to have worked out all the old stuff about Jamie. That's important for both of us....actually for the three of us. Funny, that we had to get to Heaven for that to happen."

"Do you know where that came from, 'Our Lord does all things for each,' the quote Columba gave you?" Laurence said.

I shook my head.

Heaven's Missing Wing

"Perhaps something else?" Cloud said. "I have delectable choco-late chip cookies—fresh from the oven."

"Sounds good, Cloud." Laurence said. "And maybe some milk for the cherubs."

"The angel Marie approaches." Cloud said and the door disappeared.

I jumped up and hugged Marie. "Marie, you'll never know how much your perfume helped us."

"So glad. Tell me."

A steaming pile of cookies arrived.

"Do we have to worry about calories here?" Joe said.

"No!" we all said in unison.

"See, now that's my idea of heaven."

"Let's catch you and Marie up on Hannah's story." Laurence said. "Oh, Marie, this is Joe. Joe, Marie."

They nodded at each other, then Marie said, "Tony and I were talking about all of this last night. Talking and wondering what hap-pened after we saw you."

"Well, let's start from the beginning." I said.

"A very good place to start," said Laurence, and I laughed. I had missed him.

But back to business. "You'll remember Hannah's wing disap-peared during a basketball game. We now think that was some type of Black Magic—a sleight of hand trick so fast none of us could see."

"Black Magic—in Heaven?" said Joe.

"Marie, tell him where you got the perfume." Laurence said.

Marie looked around. "I know this will seem strange to you but—"

"—nothing seems strange to us anymore." I said.

"Well, there's a group of female angels who grew up in the Quarter, the French Quarter. They were always good Catholics, but lived close to other women who practiced voodoo. The two groups of women were friendly. Because of this friendship, my Catholic friends know how to make certain . . . potions. I was afraid for Hannah and asked them for

CHAPTER THIRTY-ONE

Soon we were zipping over the Zion clouds. Joe definitely had this flying thing down. He was going to do great when he moved on to tackle ankle wings and other refinements.

My old door dissolved before I could knock.

"Welcome, Madam. And it's fascinatingly good to have you here, Master Joe." Cloud said. "What refreshments may I serve?"

Laurence came bounding into the room. "Welcome, welcome. So good to see you, Joe. I'm sure Claire's told you more about our trip."

"Cloud, ice cold lemonade would be fantastic. I'm afraid I haven't told him everything. I asked him about all of us living together, and he agreed to come over, and so, here we are."

"Wonderful. So good to hear it." said Laurence. "Hannah is playing outside with Tiffany, but I know she'll be thrilled. Please, sit. How was your trip over?"

"Sweet. This flying stuff is kind of fun," Joe said.

"Saw Regina in the market. She told me. Very impressive, Joe. And Claire, Marie is coming over soon."

"Fabulous. I want to thank her for that obnoxious scent."

"You're going to thank her for something that smelled bad?" Joe said.

I waved to him that I would explain later. Chilly lemonades plopped down for each of us.

of hope, love, and faithful guidance—they took our feet and hands in perfect paths. Plus, amazing spun gold and wool undergarments that helped us cope with the frigid place."

Laurence stood up to pour a glass of milk for himself and Joe. Marie and I declined. "What she's not telling you is that the gate is also known as the Wicked Way and is a very dangerous place. Easy to get in, but very hard to get out of again. But Claire and Hannah did it."

"How did you manage, honey?"

Bam! The back door slammed before I could answer Joe's question. Tiffany and Hannah ran into the room.

"Cookies!" Tiffany said with a little scream.

"Yeay!" Hannah answered with the same volume.

"Girls." I said in a quiet voice. "We're telling the story of the wing. Do you want to join us?"

They looked at each other as they quickly grabbed a cookie.

"Will you be mad if I just stay for a little while, Claire?" Hannah poured herself a glass of milk.

"Of course not."

"Hannah's pretty much told me everything." Tiffany said while she balanced a plate of two cookies and a glass of milk.

They sank back into a love seat.

"Where are you in what happened?" Hannah said.

"In the Wicked Way."

"Ick, the horrible part."

"Well, not really, though, because you were strong and we flew out with your wing."

Everyone clapped. "Amen." said Marie.

"Have you told them, er, everything?"

"They know we had a tough time, sweetie."

"It's okay," Joe said. "You're back. You have your wing. That's all that matters."

a scent to ward off evil spirits. That was the awful smelling stuff I gave her. "

"But it worked, Marie." I said.

"How?"

"When we went to the South West Gate—"

"You went there! It's off limits, that was so dan—"

"Calm down, Marie, we had to go, I can explain. Anyway, when we went, this horrible creature told Hannah to stay away from her because she was wearing a bad scent. After she said that, I realized it had a powerful purpose."

"I've always been told that, guess we know now for sure."

"But start at the beginning, Claire." said Joe. "After the wing was missing, what happened?"

"Not too long after, Marie and Tony visited us. Tony was upset about a curious incident at the border crossing where he works."

"I'd worked there long ago." said Laurence. "I thought it sounded suspicious, this gentleman not claiming bags, bags going missing, and told Tony to run it up the flag pole. He had."

"Later I met Gabriel, he said Corporate was aware of this."

"Really? Wait 'till I tell Tony." Marie said.

"Gabriel told me that I had to go with Hannah as she searched for her wing, and that we'd receive clues along the way. The first one took us to the Heavenly Host."

"Don't they float around and sing all the time?" Joe said.

Laurence laughed. "Something like that, but they have powerful gifts, too. One of them gave Hannah two earfuls."

"Wow," said Marie.

"I just read about those in the *Guide*." said Joe.

"Hannah sang with both of them at the South West Gate." I said. "She was very brave."

"Where else did you go?" Marie said.

"The Castles and a monastery just outside the gate. Laurence flew Hannah to the monastery. They gave us gifts, too. Boots and gloves